Spirit of Sunrise

SPIRIT OF SUNRISE

Selected talks by

MICHAEL CECIL · ALAN HAMMOND
GEORGE EMERY · THEODORE BLACK
JAMES WELLEMEYER · ROGER DE WINTON
WILLIAM BAHAN

MITRE PRESS
52 Lincoln's Inn Fields · London

© EMISSARIES OF DIVINE LIGHT, 1979
The Mitre Press (Fudge & Co. Ltd.),
52 Lincoln's Inn Fields, London WC2A 3NW

ISBN 0 7051 0270 X (hardback)
ISBN 0 7051 0271 8 (paperback)

Cover Design by Michael Gress and Raymond Mickelic

Made and printed in Great Britain by
Hazell Watson & Viney Ltd,
Aylesbury, Bucks

CONTENTS

FOREWORD

The Sunrise Ranch community near Loveland, Colorado, is the core of a worldwide body of men and women whose purpose is to reveal the truth of Life in each moment of living. Quality of character is the primary concern of those involved; what is expressed must be true to the nature of this character – strong, noble, compassionate and balanced.

The seven contributors to this book have all dwelt on Sunrise Ranch and are leaders in this rapidly expanding organism. They, with thousands of others, consider themselves members of a great family, a family to whom all belong as the true character is known and expressed in living.

This book consists of the transcripts of extemporaneous public talks given during the past several years. They have been selected to introduce you to the true nature and processes of Life, and also that you may be assisted in discovering the truth of yourself so that you might move into position to fulfil those unique purposes for which you are on earth.

The spirit of Sunrise is not limited to Sunrise Ranch, obviously, for it is in fact the ultimate force in human affairs. It is the spirit of Life itself, which is available for expression by anyone, anywhere, anytime.

MICHAEL CECIL is the son of Lord Martin Cecil, Director of the Society of Emissaries.

Mr. Cecil's home has always been at 100 Mile House, B.C., Canada, where his administrative abilities have had ample scope for development. He has been a cattle rancher and director of a number of businesses. He has for a number of years coordinated the Emissary community at 100 Mile House. This has entailed offering leadership and guidance on a day-to-day basis to over 120 people who are concerned to exemplify dynamic harmony in collective living.

Business management, ranching, building, nutrition, public speaking are just some of the fields in which he has demonstrated specific leadership, and he is presently responsible for supervising the expanding Emissary program throughout the world.

100 MILE LODGE—
AGREEMENT IN ACTION

Michael Cecil

There are a lot of communal groups around these days. This has become the thing to do in many parts of the world, particularly with young people. The feeling is, on the part of many people, that the society in which they live is somehow not adequate or not right, and the attempt is made to strike out and do something different. Generally speaking, though, we find, apart from a few of the traditional religious communities, that these attempts are pretty short-lived. Our particular group has been here since 1948, growing from five people to over a hundred now. We have found, as I think is true of any grouping of people who have managed to live together and maintain a lively, creative atmosphere for any extended period of time, that there has to be a unifying factor which isn't arbitrarily imposed. I mentioned various religious communities that we all know of: one will find in many of those situations that the binding element is arbitrary control. There are many dos and don'ts: 'Thou shalt not smoke'; 'Thou shalt not drink'; 'Thou shalt get up at six o'clock in the morning.' These seem to be necessary in order to maintain some kind of orderliness and direction to things.

We have found that the only real point of agreement is spiritually based. It is not an externally based thing. Many communities today are concerned with getting together because they'd like to go into organic foods or something of the sort. Nothing of this nature motivates us. Actually we do grow organic foods, but for a different reason. It isn't the external elements that are so important, rather a common concern amongst those who are here to let the qualities of real manhood and womanhood dominate in daily experience.

Now, everyone talks about integrity, honesty, patience and things of this nature. Everyone will agree that such qualities are lovely, but in the world in which we live they don't really seem to have too much application except as one may think about them on Sunday or something. Our concern is to let those qualities, which we feel are actually inherent in everyone, dominate in what is said and in what is done in our experience. Because we have this common point of orientation we have a basis then for agreeing about any external thing. It is quite a different experience when you have a wide variety of people who have rigidly set ideas about this, that and the other thing and who individually seek to maintain those rigidly held ideas in the face of everyone else. Where there is that kind of rigidity of attitude there is certain to be an explosion sooner or later. People get together with the best of intentions and then very shortly the whole project collapses. But where there is a concern that what is right in life predominate, it becomes easy to work out the details of everyday living – how you are going to eat, how you are going to live, how you are going to do this or that. No problem!

As I say, when the group started here it was quite small – about five or six people – and just gradually has grown over the years. Many, many people would like to join us and if we opened the doors to all and sundry we'd probably have several thousand on our doorstep. There's a constant flow of mail, calls and visits from people wishing to join us, but primarily the initial desire on the part of people is to join a 'groovy commune.' They really haven't a clue as to the basis of cohesion. We do look over those who wish to join us quite carefully. Many visitors come, and we welcome that. It's fine for people to come and see what we're doing. It also gives us a chance to see how they're doing and whether they really do have a relationship with us, a feeling of empathy. If there is, then perhaps something will build and in due course perhaps this one or that one will come to be with us.

I might just point to some of the things we do and the view we have towards them. One thing of course is work. I think Gibran said something about work being love made visible. I think for most people that view isn't the fact. They work because they have to; if they don't they'll starve. As far as we are concerned we recognize that the things that are done with our hands are a means for expressing our integrity, expressing our inherent nobility and strength. We need a medium through which to express this and so we happily do what needs to be done.

About half the people in our group work in the town of 100 Mile House and participate in various business activities there. The other half or so live and work right here in the maintenance of the home, from the standpoint of cooking, cleaning, building, tending gardens, milking goats, and so forth. The ladies – I suppose there would be about forty of them – do have a point of coordination in the person of Marcia Marks (the mayor's wife, incidentally). She makes out a schedule every day as to what all of them should do. It would be nice just to leave things easy so that people could do what they felt like doing, but with that many people around and with a substantial number of things to be looked after, it simply isn't practical. There has to be coordination. And our people, whether women or men, find themselves doing certain jobs for a while and then perhaps something else for another period of time. I think anyone who has been here for a number of years finds out that they become capable in many fields. It's quite an educational experience, a university in living you might say. Every day the ladies look at their schedule to see whether they are going to cook dinner, or clean, or wash out some toilet bowls, or make some beds, or work in the garden, or whatever. All these things need to be attended to in a spirit of love, in a spirit of joy, because here's an opportunity for the person to express creatively. The same is true of the men. Each morning after breakfast the men get together in the log building next door and various activities are looked at for the day. Then the men go out to do those things, in recognition that the real basis for our experience here is a spiritual one, where there is a concern that the expression of word, thought and action be as true and clear as possible in the way of integrity, of honorableness.

We all get together several times a week. At those times we're joined by other people in the area who are interested in what we're doing. There is, incidentally, another sizable group whose members live and work in the village itself, and there are still others around the local countryside as well. At these special gatherings we give specific thought to the spiritual approach to life. This is something which has immediate application, something that we can see in terms of the actions that need to take place, of the inter-relationships between us, of the discomforts or the pleasures or whatever that we find amongst ourselves. Here we have a chance to look with greater clarity at such matters, to see how better we may express ourselves, how much taller we may stand.

These meetings usually take the form of lectures. On Sundays Lord Martin Cecil addresses the group, when he is here. As a point of interest for you, there is a book currently on sale called *Being Where You Are*, which is a series of sixteen lectures that he gave extempore, some of them here, in the last year or two. The book gives something of an idea of the approach that we take and the manner in which we handle things. If work is to be love made visible there needs to be a consideration of love, and the nature of it in the expression of life. We do this regularly.

So there is spiritual food. We are concerned with physical food too, obviously. It's said that the North American eats about 1500 pounds of food a year! So here's an area that needs to take our attention to some extent at least, and if we are concerned to be right in our living in all respects then we are concerned about rightness in handling food, in cooking, in growing, in the way it's eaten. We do have a fairly extensive vegetable garden here. An outstanding gardener, with a tremendous amount of experience in organic gardening, is in charge of this operation. We also have an orchard near Kamloops, B.C., where there is another large garden as well, about three or four acres. We keep our chickens there; also a few sheep and some bees. At 100 Mile House we operate a cattle ranch, which surrounds our communal property, and we are concerned with organic growing and with raising our cattle in a balanced way. We have that provision available for our own use of course, as well as it being a business in its own right. We have a friend right now who is salmon fishing for us off the west coast of B.C. We have friends in the Okanagan Valley (famous for fruit growing) who either have their own orchards or know of people who have orchards with the kind of fruit that we're looking for. So one way or another we have a very ample provision.

Our concern about organics is really a concern for something far larger. It's not that we think it's groovy to eat organic foods and get our hands in organic soil and grow organic worms, but because there is a recognition that there is order to life, a rhythm to life. In this field, as in any other, we feel that it is our responsibility to acknowledge that fact, and to move with that natural order and rhythm as though life really knows what it's doing already! We humans have given ourselves a lot of abuse over the years. That we have survived is mostly not of our own doing! Life is both indomitable and very clever in keeping us on our feet. So the more respect we have in that direction the better off we are, and one way we acknowledge that is in relation to the handling of our food.

Many in our group are connected with a number of businesses in the village of 100 Mile House. We were here first and the town has grown up with us. Various businesses and community affairs have developed, and we have found ourselves right in the midst of these things, carrying various responsibilities. We have been eager for such responsibilities, recognizing that it's not enough to talk about spiritual values. People say, 'Well, it's all right for you. There you are in a commune back in the bush, away from the dog-eat-dog world. *You* can be spiritual, but I have to make my living. I have to work things out in this wretched situation.' Well, we all find ourselves in many wretched situations! But the point is not to see them as wretched but to see them as a means for expressing this real value which all of us have to express.

We operate Red Coach Inn, Red Coach Esso and Red Coach Bakery; Tip Top Radio and TV; the Free Press, a weekly paper; Pioneer Building Supply; Pioneer Construction Company; Cariboo Accounting. We have a hand in South Cariboo Realty and Insurance; we run Bridge Creek Estate, which operates the cattle ranch, various rentals around town and also the agency for the Inland Natural Gas Company; Hundred Mile Water Utilities (we supply the water for the village); Bridge Creek Holding Company, which has to do with the development of subdivisions from ranch land which immediately surrounds the village; and, more recently,

Coach House Square, which is the beginning of a shopping center. These for the most part are companies operating in their own right, and the management of them is supplied from 100 Mile Lodge.

It is from these areas of course that our family finances come. Various ones in the communal group provide their labor to the different businesses. Take Red Coach Inn as an example. There are about forty or fifty employees, and perhaps ten of those are part of our group here; the rest are hired from the area round about. And those ten people then contract their labor at whatever the going rate is for the jobs in which they are working, and that returns to our 'communal pot,' you might say. This helps to buy us blankets and electricity and building materials for continued expansion and provides us with funds to keep ourselves clothed. We have an interesting situation to work out in keeping a balance between the number of people who have jobs in the village and the number who attend to affairs within the family here. It is easy to overbalance one way or another. If almost everyone's working out then the few who remain are overextending themselves to feed the rest – or you can go to the other extreme, where everyone's sitting around pulling weeds out of the garden and there's no money coming in.

As I say, while the financial provision is important, it isn't the primary reason for doing the things that we do in the community. It's all a part of this proving ground for the experience of inner worth; that's the only thing that really matters. None of us would be here if it weren't for that. A person interested in money probably could do much better financially in other places.

We have about twenty-five children in our group here. Those of school age attend the local schools. Some people have said, 'Why don't you have your own school if you think society is not what it should be?' Our feeling is that the necessity is to learn how to handle oneself in the world as it is. It's not a matter of getting out of society or trying to change the world, to overthrow the government or something, but of learning how to handle the situation as it is with uprightness, with joy and with ease. It can be done. Why not start right away? Now, our children go to school and are thereby exposed to many influences. They need to have that contact with the larger world. We're delighted with that, realizing that if the parents actually are experiencing anything that's worthwhile then the substance of experience is present in the home and it is the primary influence in their lives. So there is no need for imposition. What an atrocious thing this idea of arbitrary imposition is! It just indicates a feeling of weakness on the part of the person who applies it. If something is really valid it's going to stand anyway, and it's going to have lasting influence.

You saw the swimming pool we have back here and perhaps you also saw the tennis court. We have in the basement of one of our buildings a pool table and in another a sauna bath. There is a children's play yard and playhouse. Some have horses. There are all kinds of things for the children to do. Of course it is our concern that the children should play their part in the operation of our community here too. There is some responsibility to assume, many things to be learned as they grow; not only how to do things but how to relate to people.

Health is something I might touch on. I think the local doctors have sometimes been suspicious of us because they don't find us crowding into their offices. Let me underline here that we like our doctors very well. They certainly fill a vital need. We have recognized however that to the extent a person does begin to move in harmony with the natural ebb and flow of life he finds himself much healthier. If we eat healthy food it does help us to be healthy. That's part of our concern. Also, if a person isn't thinking that the world is against him, that does have an effect on his well-being. He may not have ulcers and he may not have various other ill conditions physically which otherwise he would have to contend with! And so, while there are difficulties to be handled from a physical standpoint from time to time, I think our problems are far less than the average.

One of the areas that we appreciate is natural childbirth. My wife had a baby recently. It was a delightful experience that worked out very rapidly. It caused some anguish, I think, in the hospital because we only got there with ten minutes to spare! We could hardly imagine that it would go so easily and so fast. I think it was indicative of the experience that's available in all aspects of living when one begins to be willing to move with life and to fulfil its purposes rather than going against it in pursuit of selfish goals.

Something that is moving with us quite joyfully is music. We have a choir and we've been developing an orchestra. You will hear the string section of the orchestra tonight at your banquet. We are also into folk music. There's a dance after the banquet tonight and our locally renowned 'Range Patrol' band will be performing. So you'll hear the kind of music they make.

As I mentioned earlier, we have many visitors. And something that has taken a lot of our energy in the last few years has been to provide a facility for four-week courses in the art of living. People come from all over Canada, the United States and other countries to share in this month-long experience with us. Usually the class numbers around fifty people. We have one coming up at the end of June. Primarily, students contact us through association with people elsewhere who already know us. There are groups connected with us all over the world now – I think about 140. I particularly wanted to emphasize this because many have thought of our group here – Emissaries of Divine Light – as an isolated little venture situated in the woods in the Cariboo country, when actually it is something quite extensive.

The international headquarters, comprising a group like this, only rather larger, is located in Colorado at a place called Sunrise Ranch. Classes are also held there. Literature and other means of overall coordination go out from there. There are also other primary communities around the continent. One is at a place called Livingston Manor in upstate New York, a beautiful location; another at Epping, New Hampshire; and one at King City, Ontario, just north of Toronto. A new community is being developed just outside Aldergrove, B.C.

All of this has been working out, with an increasing number of people becoming interested in what we're doing and beginning to share in this experience, because of the direction and leadership of one man. Lord Martin Cecil came to 100 Mile House straight from the Royal Navy in 1930, as an inexperienced youth. He built the Lodge, never before having lifted a hammer. He calls it a monument to his inexperience, but really it is quite solid and has been a beautiful provision for us! He learned how to run a cattle and sheep ranch, a general store, the local post office, etc. He came here just at the beginning of the depression, when there was a good deal of hardship one way or another, and, I think, developed as many patches on his pants as anyone else around here. By that particular experience, which many people went through in those days, he was brought very consciously to a realization of the need for man to have values that are other than material. Many people at that time did have some realization of this, but it tended to fade when things got better again in the material sense. However, it did provide a point of impetus for him, and in his search for a deeper meaning in life he came in contact with a man called Lloyd Meeker, who had a remarkable spiritual insight. They found an immediate agreement in these matters about which I have been speaking: the concern for the expression of integrity in life.

Emissaries of Divine Light is the name that has been used for our program and on first sight this looks like certain religious names with which you are doubtless familiar. It tends to be pigeonholed very quickly into the same category. But just look at the name for a minute: Emissaries of Divine Light. An emissary is one who carries a message. And what is divine light other than the integrity, the real values of life that are inherent in man? And so an Emissary of Divine Light is anyone who is willing to put his inner worth first and express that in his life, not to lay it on anyone but just to be true to himself, true to his own being. In the experience and realization of that, there is something light about such a person. He seems to have a good deal of fun and joy in living, and that is the light. It's not something that is forcefully laid on anyone else, but is presumably simply his own experience. So it is such an exemplification through Lord Martin Cecil that has drawn response and interest from many people in many places. Here is a man who through his own experience in living over many years has exemplified the finest quality of character. He has lived it out. It's the living that tells the tale. There are a lot of noble words spoken in our world but who is actually doing anything? We are concerned here with the wisdom and direction that he has provided over the years to really live life nobly. And if in fact we have found some genuine agreement together, we feel that this is a pilot scheme which is of extreme significance to all the world. We're not going out to arbitrarily sell it and we're not just keeping it to ourselves, but we feel that if in fact creative changes can happen in people so that they love life and are masters of their experiences and have a light shining in their eyes always, this is extremely attractive. This does begin to influence the immediate environment in the world around.

I have been thinking of the talk we heard yesterday at lunch about the United Nations' 'Habitat' project and what world government is going to do about all the problems of society over the next numbers of years. Well I bless the sincerity and the energy of many people in seeking to turn the world around into a more harmonious and positive direction, but I know from experience here that you can do nothing in the external sense that is really going to mean a thing until people are turned around inside themselves. The world is a mirror of the consciousness of its people and it is futile indeed to try to scrub away the ugly face you see in the mirror. But you can discover how to put a smile on it so easily! That is our concern here.

A lecture given to the Convention of B.C. Community (Weekly) Newspaper Association Publishers, June 14, 1975, at 100 Mile House, B.C., Canada.

SPIRITUAL CONSCIOUSNESS

Michael Cecil

Looking around the world today, we see an increasing number of major difficulties in every field of human experience. Over the course of history attempts have been made to resolve human problems in a very specific way. These days it is all summed up in the word *involvement*. Many believe that the way to resolve problems is to get hold of them and fight them to the ground. Whether we're looking at world affairs or whether we're looking at the individual, this is generally the approach used. I'm sure that all here present have had personal experience!

After all, what else would we do when faced with a problem if we did not try to resolve and dispose of it? It seems to require involvement. It seems to require our one-pointed attention. That kind of approach can be referred to as material consciousness. Let us consider the matter of spiritual consciousness, which is the alternative. Recently I have been reading a book called *The Inner Game of Tennis*. It has something to do with tennis but basically it concerns the psychology of learning. It's written by a tennis pro who noticed, after some experience, that the harder his students tried the more difficult they found it to succeed. He also observed that those who played the game well, who happened to be on their game at the time, were usually playing in terms that might be described as 'playing out of their minds'; in other words they weren't trying. There was relaxation here and something else was taking control. I think this man has a very good awareness in that particular field of what is required. It is obvious, by looking at world affairs, that the more we try to solve our problems the more problems we have and the further away we get from solutions in relation to them. However, very often when we give up on our problems then they begin to work out. Usually we won't give up until we have no alternative, when we get forced into a corner perhaps, so that there is no way out; then finally we say, 'I give up! It's hopeless!' We step back from the situation in that moment and immediately the thing begins to work out. This indicates that there is a simple alternative to the usual material attempt to beat down our problems.

While I'm not here to talk about tennis, I must say that this particular pro found the solving of various bad habits in this field of tennis most readily came about not by fighting with bad habits but by allowing a current of energy to be directed toward a new approach which then became so dominant that the old way simply ceased to exist very shortly. Here is something available to all of us: the need to stand back from involvement in those areas of experience which we had thought most important to us and which therefore seemed to require intense concentration.

In our part of the country we recently had a strike of concrete ready-mix operators. While this strike was going on, many building contractors had to do their own concrete work and of course sometimes those who worked in such jobs were not too familiar with the process. On one particular job there was a Pakistani throwing cement and gravel into a cement mixer, and the cement mixer was going around. When he was heaving and hauling the gravel he tripped and fell in. Because he was going around inside the cement mixer he couldn't get it turned off. His voice could be heard coming out of the mouth of the cement mixer, 'Help! Help! I'm in very big trouble!' And while he was down in there trying to get out, two of his associates wandered by. They were Irish. The Irish like to lean on their shovels, so they were watching this spectacle when the foreman came along and said, 'What's going on here?' And the Irishmen said, 'The Pakistani is in the cement mixer.' So the foreman said, 'Well don't just stand there. Give him a hand, give him a hand!' So the two Irishmen applauded. But the Pakistani was still in the cement mixer!

We will diagram the cement mixer.

This is very apt – relative to human experience in life. The cement mixer is going around, down one side and up the other,

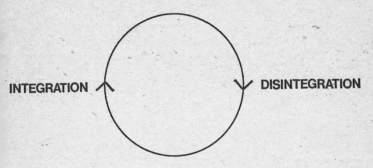

and our problem is that we all tend to fall into the cement mixer. That is what happens when we become involved in our experiences. On the one side we have what we might call disintegration going on, something that's going down; on the other side we have what we could call integration, something going up. We like things that are going up, and feel that we are making progress, so we give that a boost, try to keep it moving. But then the things that are falling apart we don't like so much, so we are busy trying to patch that up. Where are you going to get your footing from? You are involved in this thing and it's going around, you are spinning around with centrifugal force. You are plastered against the side of the machine! Why? Because you are involved in what is going on. You are involved in the external world of your senses for one thing, and you have feelings about this, concepts and bodily involvements in various ways, so that you're deeply engrossed in this cycle that is going around, trying to hold back what is falling apart and trying to push what is going up. What is going up reaches a point where it begins to come down, and if you help it up too much, well it's going to come down all the faster. And then if you try to prevent what's coming down from doing so, its eventual participation in integration is inhibited. How mixed up we get! We pass judgment on what is going on, and we don't really understand.

This is the problem. Because we are involved we can't see what is going on. Then we try to work out a philosophy of life. Everyone has a different one, depending where he happens to be in the cement mixer. There are all kinds of religious philosophies and metaphysical philosophies, sociological philosophies, economic philosophies. A number of people may get together and say that their philosophies are somewhat compatible. Others find themselves in conflict, just depending where they happen to be positioned on the spinning circle. This does describe what is occurring in the human experience. There is a cycle on the move. Man inside the cement mixer is symbolic of the fact that he is a part of the action that is going on. He seemingly can't avoid that. In this sense our bodies, our minds, our feeling realms, are part and parcel of what is occurring in the material world. We can't avoid that. This is one of the problems that tends to plague us. We think we are inevitably locked in to the cycle that's under way, and there is an underlying feeling of hopelessness and frustration about it. There's a sensing somehow that our experience should be more than we have known, and yet, being caught up in this thing that's grinding around, there really isn't much hope. What future is there in going around in a cement mixer? You may be inclined to try to stop the thing but then that is no good either because once the cement begins to settle down in the container and solidifies you can't move at all. So, better to spin around as best you can and glean a few frail blessings from what is occurring than to solidify and experience nothing!

To escape from a fate worse than death! 'Help! Help! I'm in very big trouble!' The whole reason for the cement mixer going around is to throw substance to the outside, but right in the center there's a quiet point. This can symbolize where we really should be at. Now, whether one is thinking of the movement of the cycles of life in relation to the world as a whole or whether one is thinking of this in terms of one's personal experience it is all one and the same thing, on differing scales. Looking at this from the standpoint of our personal experience, we have a symbol of our own human bodies and the experience that we go through in our lives day by day. There is a cycle moving, unfolding. We feel aches and pains; we have various things coming into our consciousness, hopes and joys and so forth. If we are all wrapped up in that then we really don't know what's going on. All we can do is hope to organize those feelings and experiences in some way so that it all settles down a bit. We need to realize that in the core of our experience there is a point to which we may orient. This is the beginning of wisdom and serenity, and therefore the beginning of vision. We begin to see what is actually going on, but only to the degree that we cease being involved in what is churning around. We begin to move in towards the center and away from the inevitable action.

Now, there are those of course who have sensed something of this and there has been the feeling of the need to get away from it all – some 'sages' disappearing into the hills, where for the next fifty years they contemplate their navels and let the world go hang! There is some sensing that there must be a place where a person may come to rest, but it isn't a physical place. There is nothing in the external sense that can be done to achieve this. Life is moving on, so we need to give up and come into the center. That is the only solution for that Pakistani. The Irishmen wouldn't give him a hand, so a person does finally need to come to the point where he can say, 'All my trying, all my desire to reach some goal, to get into better shape, to find out answers to life, to find fulfilment, is just simply not going to work.' They say that hope springs eternal in the human breast. If it does we will remain churning forever, because we think we're going to be able to work it out somehow, sometime. Giving up sounds like very negative advice, but true, in order to become still in oneself. The cement mixer is an apt symbol in another way because the present moment is represented by that central point, and on the periphery there is a cycle that has been happening for as long as we can remember and for a long time before our immediate memory too, but is down inside us as conditioning from a traumatic, cataclysmic past.

I began to realize the other day that hopes for the future are all indication of involvement in the past, because expectations for the future all must spring from the past experience. Also, in thinking of what is going to happen, one has already conditioned it from the past by the time it arrives! What is happening now is happening now and has nothing to do with the future or with the past. One needs to be sufficiently present to discover what that is. We think we can't get away from the past. This is a good part of our involvement in this spinning action. After all, for thousands of years man has had certain views on life. For example, he is afraid of what usually is referred to as God. He thinks: 'There is something out there that is bigger than I am.' There is always an apprehension based in experiences which mankind has gone through back along the way – traumatic, cataclysmic experiences – and this is seared into the mass subconscious. We as individuals share in that. We come forward with this apprehension deeply ingrained. Also, humanity in many ways has carried a great frustration through lack of experience of fulfilment, and there is a fundamental resentment present in everyone. Who is there in this world that actually feels that everything is perfect in his experience, that he is at peace with the world, there is nowhere to go, there is no future to carve out, there is nothing to be attained? Such a state is most unusual! People are resentful because they inherently know that they should be, and could be, more than they are. They sense that there is a larger experience to be known.

This shows up on the tennis court and everywhere else. A person makes a bad shot and he immediately begins to chastise himself: 'I'm just not in form today.' If he keeps doing it he says, 'My grandmother could play better,' or other less seemly words. The inclination immediately is toward self-blame, an inability to separate himself from what is going on so that he can act creatively with respect to the problem. This tendency is well established, so that whenever any pressure comes on immediately blame arises, criticism, condemnation, which all reflect ultimately on the person himself. But for as long as he can do it he will place it on someone else or on circumstances. There are so many in the world who are adept at this! If ever you see anyone complaining I would suggest that that person is complaining about himself, because he himself feels unhappy, unable to cope, and therefore is hunting for something to give him some slight sense of rationalization for his misery. If we are ever inclined to blame others, to feel resentful about anything, we should shut up! Criticism and resentment spring so quickly to the lips. It is all indication that we are spinning around and crying out, 'Help! Help! I'm in very big trouble!'

This is a double bind, because we feel frustrated and resentful due to the fact that we haven't discovered the fulness of our potential, and yet we cannot find the fulness of our potential as long as we are frustrated and resentful. So how do you get out of it? Simply because we don't need to be controlled by our feelings. If we are used to spinning around we are all locked up, one way or another, with the material world – our own bodies, our own feelings, our own thoughts, that are part and parcel of the moving cycle. But if we face the fact that we don't need to be in any way controlled by our feelings we begin to move into the central point of stillness. We have the choice. The tennis player who clears his inability to function adequately on the tennis court is he who has, in that field at least, begun to be impartial in the matter and therefore let the natural rhythm of life begin to act through him in this particular circumstance. So it is with all of life. We already have the ability to function perfectly in the present moment, to do whatever it is that is necessary to be in balance in the present moment.

It is certainly not a matter of a person who has been playing tennis badly rushing euphorically down the court saying, 'I am a perfect tennis player,' because that is not facing what is happening in the present. He has been flubbing his shots and so he needs to face that fact, but in a way which is not involved. It is his involvement, his self-judgment, his trying, his attempt to resolve the problem, that retains it. We need to face things as they are, we need to observe what is actually occurring, but we are no longer caught up in it. We simply observe and say in effect, 'Well isn't that interesting! Maybe if I did this things would work out better.' One is in no sense fighting with the problem; simply facing it and allowing the current of life which is present to work.

A good example is that of a cat stalking a bird. A bird will be feeding on the ground and the cat is creeping towards it with intent to pounce. Do you think the cat is working it all out intellectually speaking? 'Now there are only three feet three inches left. If I gather my feet up under me and tense my muscles so much, and hold my tail straight out and my whiskers like that, and then leap forward, I'll get him.' If he does that he's going to miss, isn't he? Did he think it all out? Of course not! You might say it is a reflex action. The body, given the chance to do what is necessary in the circumstance at hand, will tend to do that with very slight guidance. This just indicates the fact that all the design and all the controls necessary to enable natural and easy rhythmic function in relation to what is occurring in life are already present with us. It stands to reason, when we stop to think about it, doesn't it? What about our own bodies? What a complex process is under way just in this moment in you listening to my voice! Consider those sound waves entering your head through your ears and going through a very intricate mechanism which touches certain nerve centers in your brain, which is translated then into certain impulses, and finally they work through into thought processes so that you understand what is going on. What a marvelous thing! We think not at all about it. It's automatic to us. So many things that occur in this regard are just there. How would the baby ever walk if it had to work it all out with a slide rule? With little effort it gradually reaches the time when it can stand and make off down the room – and not at three months old, when proud parents would like it to walk, but when it fits in the natural unfolding rhythm of its own cycle of life.

To come back to that central point is the experience of spiritual consciousness. The realm of material consciousness is in involvement with the churning cement mixer. There is nothing wrong with that world, but it is our deep attachment to it that has been the problem. Rightly we belong at the central point of spiritual consciousness. That is not an airy-fairy thing – 'Maybe if I get more religious, if I believe something more, I'll be able to understand what life is all about.' It is simply a matter of being here in the present moment and unattached to what is going on. We all have had occasional experience of this. The question is, How consistent is it? It is as the individual allows something of this to occur in him moment by moment by moment that understanding comes as to the direction in which life is unfolding.

Now, I said that the cement mixer is going around, the rhythms of life are unfolding in our own bodies and in the world at large, and if we are not involved in this but are at the center of things, we see, as it were, a movie going by; life is passing us. This is the exact opposite to what is usually thought of, that we have to make progress, we have to go from here to there. We then trudge right out of the present moment! We're caught up in trying to reach a fulfilment that never can be attained. It is good really to come to rest here, now, because only in this present moment is there the possibility of the experience of life.

People are always looking for the elixir of eternal life, a kind of snake oil for maintaining the experience of youth. It's right here! It's only because we get out of the present moment that we begin to die and disintegrate. As I say, all the energy expended in our society is geared to trying to hold together the decaying body of humanity itself, which has left the present – maybe not entirely, because there are still a few last gasps of breath going on. Only in the present can we know life. To be linked up with that is to have a basis for wisdom, to have an eternal balance, to cope with all things that occur, because one is at the source of all that is occurring. People don't understand what's going on in the world because they're all caught up in galloping around with it. In the cement mixer where does the focus of power come from? It comes from the hub which is hooked up with the motor. To be there is to understand and to be one with the source of movement. If it's moving out through you it's not moving you. There is a difference.

Spiritual consciousness is down-to-earth, immediate. People talk about how they can't be concerned with spiritual things because they have to be practical in life, when in actual fact everyone is already living in a world of make-believe. For one thing, everyone, as I say, is living in the past. You know, things have been going around and around for a long time. We can diagram this central point. Extend it over time and it becomes a long line, a series of points. This moment and this moment and this moment and this moment go together to make a long line. Then we have the cement mixer going around over time, and we have a cycle appearing.

We have diagramed the history of the world! Cement mixer antics! We have the central point of being from which all life emerges. It is not moving. It is stable in time but the cycles of life go around: spring comes, winter comes; things grow, things decay.

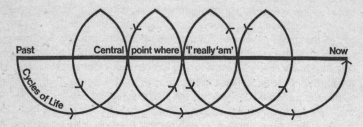

That's all very natural and necessary within the material rhythm. We are too dizzy to understand what's happening as long as we are going around with those cycles. But why be out there? Because in this present moment I can certainly say, 'I am!' To be really here is to be linked up with all that is going on without going around with it and to understand the reasons for everything that has ever happened — which makes sense, really, doesn't it, because if this central point today is really the same as this point yesterday, and this point all the way back, then we are linked with the fundamental source which lies behind all that has occurred.

I was a specialist in history. I learned all about history. If you haven't, I'll tell you it's boring and mostly unintelligible, because you can look at it from the American point of view or from the Canadian point of view, where I come from, or from the English point of view that I was taught, and you end up with all kinds of conflicting material. Nobody really knows, because they're all positioned around the walls of the cement mixer. Only when we come to rest at the center can we see how it all fits together, and it's quite different than anyone thought. A wise man once said, 'Before Abraham was, I am.' I have already diagramed this, 'I am.' I am at the central point now. Because this is the same point as the one more than four thousand years ago where Abraham was, I can go back before that too. This wise man called Jesus did, in His own experience of life, what I am talking about. It is not a religious trip, simply the experience of practical living in a world that has historically refused really to live in the present but has been all wrapped up by reason of feeling involvement in what has gone on in the past.

You've no doubt heard about the Turks and the Greeks fighting each other over Cyprus. The fact is that the Turks and the Greeks have been fighting for a long time. The Greeks and Trojans did battle around 800 B.C., and the Greeks surrounded the city of Troy. Being quite cunning, they worked out something with a wooden horse and got inside the city and took away a high-priced maiden from the Trojans (who later were to become Turks) and sacked the place. Without pausing for breath almost, the Turks and the Greeks have been at it down through history, until in 1974 no Turk will trust a Greek bearing gifts. That is where that adage springs from! Because of what happened back there President Makarios of Cyprus and a gentleman called Grivas (very aptly named) were fighting hammer and tongs until General Grivas up and died, probably of an overdose of resentment. If you were to ask people why this is happening now they'd have some explanation for it, but fundamentally it has to do with feeling involvement brought forward from the past. People say, 'We can't help being resentful. We have our likes and dislikes. You have to put up with us.' That's why we have wars in the world. People are unwilling to change, but they expect everyone else to do so.

However, in a moment we can sever the control over us by our feeling realms, so that we actually become free agents. It is feasible for everyone of us present in this room *really* to be here. The actual fact is that the effects that are appearing now in our circumstances are the result of what is going on now. Life is of the present moment and is the motivating force behind all effects. Thus past events such as the Trojan War do not actually form the originating compulsion behind the present hostilities in Cyprus. It is the currents of life that are moving; they may stir up ancient memories into the consciousness of the individual. In fact if we will accept life as it is here and now we may associate with it clean and fresh, so that our actions spring from our orientation in the central point. Involvements in the past are only possible when identity is out on the rim of the cement mixer. And so we have a word to say, we have a thought to think, we have an action to take, and it may be based clearly on a decision in ourselves to be true to the truth that we know now, regardless of what we feel. We may feel plenty coming up from the past as our capacities come around again in the experience of day-to-day living. Daily events may trigger things in our subconscious and tell us, 'Remember that you are always resentful with this particular thing. Just give in again. It's the only fair thing to do to yourself!' But you don't have to. There will always be something knocking on your door for a reaction but the choice is there, if you wish to remain true to your own inner point of balance. If you will simply do that, you discover increasingly that there is something magical to flow out through you that brings the whole fulfilment that men yearn for in life. It's all there waiting to come out.

That is the message of this evening. To the extent that we have been able to work together this has been our experience, because here we are in the present moment and you have been listening. What I have been saying has to emerge in accordance with what is present here now; for one thing, in accordance with what is happening in you. How could I possibly know that before I came? It is not a matter of being all set up ahead of time, so that one could just spit out a prepared message: 'Here we are again, folks. Just open your ears to this pretaped nonsense from the past.' You would be frustrated and I would be frustrated. As it is, here is the opportunity really to experience something that is fresh and new and immediate. We all have been sharing a conversation together, though you at this point are not speaking out loud. There is an interchange here, and something emerges on the basis of that, so that any one of you should be able to come up here tonight and take my place. It should be quite feasible, if we have really been talking together. You might say, 'I couldn't do that. I've never spoken in public.' Good for you! If you had you might have some illusion that you already know, and you would bring that bag from out of the past into the present because you'd feel more secure. But actually to come up here not knowing what you're going to say, that is the beginning of life, that is heaven! And that actually has to become our continual experience; we simply don't know ahead of time.

I don't mean by that that we trudge blindly into the present saying, 'All's well with the world,' sniffing a rose! We are increasingly alert to the trends that are unfolding. We see things emerging out of the mist for what they are. But we're not prejudging anything and then trying to place our bets ahead of time, because we think we know how it's going to work. That is always a very insecure experience, because when things begin to go wrong and you have your bets all set, then what are you going to do? It's much better just to play it cool, play your cards right up close. There is no need to judge anything, simply to be present, to be present with your integrity, so that the expression that is needed now is given regardless of how you feel.

How we tend to give in to all kinds of feelings that are present and let them color our action! Oh to stand away from all that and to see what is really going on, to breathe the fresh air of now, to see the colors, hear the sounds that are present now – something that most people never do. There is magic present! We have a responsibility, actually, to find how to relate to that magic, to become artists in this. And artistic expression through us moment by moment produces beauty on earth. We have a lot of sadness in this world and it's because people don't live now; they're all caught up in the circulating cement mixer. There is no need to spin any more, no need to try to stop the world, but simply to be here now in this place which is absolutely perfect and in which absolute serenity and absolute strength may be discovered.

It's a delight to share this special experience with you tonight!

A talk given at the Tucson Community Center, August 8, 1974.

AN INSIGHT INTO EMISSARY VIEWS ON LIFE

Michael Cecil

All that has been opening up in the Southwest for our program is good to see. Something is occurring all over the world, really. I'm looking forward, for example, to a conference of group leaders in England next January, those who provide a focus for the developing groups we have now in Europe and Africa. Quite specific response is beginning to emerge. Indeed, in September there will be a one-week seminar in England which I expect will be very well attended. We have groups all over the place, as many of you know, in that part of the world, all the way from Germany to Jerusalem. And we are discovering many friends in that latter part of the world, both Arab and Israeli, and other nationalities as well. There is quite a caldron boiling there, and that's just fine as far as we're concerned. In a sense the more heat there is the more friends we are likely to find! Because, as is probably true in the lives of many of you, it has been those times of heat that have brought to the fore the importance of a spiritual orientation.

So we may feel uncomfortable at certain times, and the human habit is to seek to avoid discomfort. But in fact we really should welcome it because it invariably leads us into a greater experience – if we persist in high vision – a greater experience and understanding of what really matters. As I say, the human tradition is to try to keep things more or less stabilized, comfortable. If we can arrange that, then all is well, that is heaven on earth. Only it never really seems to work out that way over too long a period. If it happens for someone over here it doesn't happen for someone else over there; maybe experiences switch after a while. But I'm sure for most of us there is some considerable awareness that heaven on earth, the state of peace on earth, is as a result of an orientation to spiritual values and not because we find some clever way of getting things to work out how we want them. I think it is the dashing of our hopes in that regard that has been the most helpful thing in our lives. To the extent that any of us still feel that we may, hopefully, get things to work out how we would like them we are bound in hell. And I know that for most people there may be a reaching out towards spiritual consciousness, spiritual values and so on, but there is still a tendency to keep a little of the old association in reserve, which can be reverted to if the going gets rough. But of course the going does get rough as long as one maintains two sets of values. And so there always seems to be reason to revert to more material and earthly orientation. For example, how strong the human conviction is of the need for personal fulfilment. That is earthly orientation. Where there has been a concern in consciousness for one's own fulfilment, one's own well-being, one's own satisfaction in some manner, it is found that spiritual orientation leads right away from that. Only because there is not a personal concern for fulfilment can there begin to be a larger awareness, a larger sense of purpose and direction. That is the thing I'm sure that has exercised our awareness to some extent. In order for an understanding of what that purpose might really be, of what the design of things really is, it is essential that we learn what it means to be present, thoroughly present.

Now, for many here present this is a well-worn concept: 'To live in the present moment is a good thing. Most people live in the future or the past.' We readily can roll that off the tongue! But what is the actual experience? To what extent have we seen the spiritual implications that are here in the present? And how much are we still captivated by fears, by feelings of shame and guilt, by feelings of urgent desire of one sort or another? In theory we say, 'Well those things aren't important.' We put them aside. But I really wonder if there aren't for most of us many fishhooks in our flesh, as it were, which tend to hold back the full force of life from really moving through us, something that when it is released is massive in its influence and massive in its experience in a personal sense.

How do you think of yourself in the external sense? Most

people, from my observation, are very strongly convinced of their own inadequacy. There may be the appearance, as one looks around, of many people who feel very proud of themselves. After all, they have this strong ego present and are busy promoting themselves, saying how wonderful they are. Of course the louder the trumpet blasts in that regard the weaker the individual really feels. He's desperately looking around for someone who will agree that he is worthwhile. The louder he blows his trumpet the less likely anyone is to agree! And then there are those who don't blow their trumpets who also feel unsure of themselves. How many here present, for example, have an appreciation for and delighted feeling about their own bodies? In my observation most people have a lot of reservations about their bodies. They feel that they're not very well equipped to do the job. They're sick or badly coordinated or they're the wrong shape – that's a very common one. How ridiculous! Just because *Playboy* magazine has set a standard for female shape, is that a reason for me or you to feel dissatisfied? Who set the standard, really? Did *Playboy* create man? I venture to say that there are many here present who have a very low opinion of themselves physically speaking. This beautiful instrument, which no humanly devised machine can match even in its most polished state, tends to be put down; feelings of shame and guilt perhaps for not having performed adequately, feelings of embarrassment. So much of the way we act relates to this sort of thing. Civilization is formed around this. And then there is the mind. That's the way it's usually referred to, isn't it? 'The mind is giving me trouble again,' as though it's some disjointed entity that will attack if we're not on the watch, an evil thing that we would be better off with if it was out of town. Yet we know that if our physical bodies weren't present we wouldn't be much good; it's just as true of our minds. What a beautiful instrument, if we are not out to lunch, if we're not ashamed and frightened and embarrassed by what we have to work with!

And if these negative attitudes are present in day-to-day function we are not living in the present moment, and we are not to that extent able to relate adequately to what life would have expressed now. We're too busy lumbering around with our grotesque convictions, and it's completely unnecessary. Until we are able to be really fully present we cannot find out in experience what this grand design is all about, what our purpose is. And I think there has been a great deal of game playing in this regard among those associating with this program. Because historically there has been so little real experience of life everyone has the habit of looking around to see what the form is, to see what the acceptable thing is. Everyone else comes to meetings twice a week, and maybe if they're really getting on they'll read Adelle Davis or Immanuel Velikovsky, perhaps go to one of our classes and live in a communal house! And if you do these things, and many more, then you will be on board the train to heaven too! But it's all completely divorced from what life really has happening now. It's not to say that there's anything wrong in coming to a meeting or living in a communal home or whatever, and Adelle Davis has some good ideas; but if you are looking around to see what the accepted concept is, and then seeking to conform to that, you simply don't know what life is all about; you never will. On the other hand there are those who get fed up with this after a while and say, 'Well I'm not going along with that stuff.' Here is a concept about the concept. The person is reacting about the way things are being done by others as though that's his own experience.

But what is life? No person can actually know until he is fully here and functional in the present, not just going along looking over his shoulder to see if he conforms or not. I would say that there are many who have received our mailings over the years who don't know what life's about. They can perhaps recite sentences and paragraphs from the mailings. Wonderful! They know all the words, and yet they have never really seen the implications that were contained there in relation to themselves, so that something new in a momentary sense actually occurred. The connection was never made.

Here's a concept for you that's commonly held: If you get ill it is thought that you must have sinned; if you are ill we all know that your emotional realm must have been out from under control, and there it is splattered all over your body! And what about death? One of these days – in spite of another concept, that if you now are associated with this program all is going to be well and you will live forever – in fact we are all going to die; and not only that, but probably as the end comes we will be ill, in pain and anguish because of it! If one has lived an effective life in spiritual expression this may still occur. What then? As you sink into your final illness will you cast away everything worthwhile you have expressed all your life to a feeling of guilt and shame because now, 'I have failed. I'm sick again.' This has been an attitude often held, incidentally, by those in positions of leadership. There is the desire to help people get well. Many have believed that that's what we're here for, to get everyone on the road to health and happiness. So much nonsense, really. The word is, of course, that we need to live in the moment, and whatever the circumstance is now let some light shine through that, regardless of the conditions. In fact the more rigorous the conditions, as I inferred earlier, the better chance there is for something of real potency to be expressed. Remember that, when you're gasping your last. Better still, remember it now!

We all have had some connection with the grim reaper at one time or another, as it related to someone else. No doubt because of the traditional views that were present with respect to death we were conscious of a certain unpleasantness associated with it. And yet some of you may have had the experience where you weren't particularly involved in such feelings of impending doom or preoccupation with sadness and were able to sense that there was something present in that experience which was actually glorious, the freeing of spirit from a twisted and limited physical form. If one is perceptive and open, unprejudiced, there is something very beautiful to be touched and known, but all too few do, because instead of looking up they look down. It's actually nothing to be anguished about but rather something to rejoice in. And this is true in everything, surely. Whatever occurs is not reason for us to be ashamed or to put ourselves down for our inadequacy, or our ugliness, or our lack of proficiency, or whatever, but simply to welcome it as it is and to let be released into it the very richest possible thing that is available to be expressed.

If we are to do this more adequately it obviously requires an openness of heart, and for the most part people have held their hearts shut to the direction in which they needed to be opened. It is the human tradition. After all, that's what the story of Adam and Eve is all about. They hid behind the bushes in the garden when, as the story says, the voice of the Lord came walking in the garden; and they stayed hidden behind the bushes, their hearts closed. And what was the key to the closure? Blame! 'It was her fault!' 'It was the snake's fault,' and all the rest. The release of blame is a large part of the key to opening the heart – the willingness to face the fact that there is no one in this present moment but oneself and life. To point the finger and say that something is standing in my way is to deny the possibilities that are actually present. The place that finger is first pointed is right at my capacities, my physical form, my mind, my emotions. And then there is a feeling of shame and it's uncomfortable and the tendency is to blame something further out. There must be someone who's in the way, and it's all his fault! But of course it isn't really true. There isn't anyone present who can prevent us from the experience of life as it really is. That is something that, although it has been acknowledged by some, in many ways hasn't been believed. We need to trust in the validity of life, to lay ourselves open to that, so that what we are actually capable of may be released. All the blocks have been right inside, not on beyond at all. There needs to be a willingness to open up. There has been very little real opening up in the innermost sense, the bringing out of one's inner self, you might say, into the light. After all, if one is to convey some light into one's momentary experience the light has to be present. If the door is shut because there is a lack of trust, then that light isn't going to come out. We may look for reasons why, but ultimately there is only one: We do not trust God, trust life itself.

So how to open up, that is the question. Of course a person says, with some genuine conviction, 'I opened up along the way and when I did I got shafted. I went to someone who looked trustworthy, thought he was a genuine guru, and I laid myself at his feet and he stepped on me.' This is generally what people think of as trust. This is what is done in our world in every field. People do this to their doctors. The body is dragged along to the local saw-bones, and the owner says, 'Something's wrong. Fix it up and send it home! I'll pay the price.' And billions of dollars go out this way. Now, I'm not saying that it isn't right to go to the doctor or whoever, but on what basis? As I say, there is an irresponsible tendency to take the lump along and lay it on the doctor's bench, have him cut it up or sew it up or fill it full of pills. It tends to be this way from the standpoint of counseling, from the standpoint of spiritual concerns as well: an attempt to find the guru and then let that person make the decisions. One is happy to indicate one's own concern and desire to do whatever is said. 'I'm so willing, just tell me what to do. I've been waiting for years for someone to give me the word,' and there are those who fall into the trap of giving the word. In many sectors of society there are those who will in all good faith, in all desire to help, say, 'Now you do this and do that and do the other thing,' and the person follows along with a certain measure of faith, and wonderful things may seem to occur, but because it wasn't that person's own experience, sooner or later there comes a great fall and disillusionment.

In this matter of trust there needs to be an element of personal responsibility. One's trust needs to be in life itself, in the spiritual quality of life, so that there is a willingness fully to open up to that. Don't take the attitude, 'Blindly I will do whatever you say.' Some will even seek out some dusty tome written years ago, read it all and learn it all by heart, quick to have faith in that external form. Actually to let some genuine action take place in oneself, that would never do! But that is the nature of true trust.

There are lots of people who say, 'Well I trust the Lord. There's no one in this stupid world I can trust, because I'll get shafted. But I trust the Lord. I pray to Him every night.' That kind of association *in absentia* doesn't mean too much. In the end we need to find a person to whom we can relate and open ourselves, not in the sense of laying ourselves on that person, but of having a counterpoint for our own opening up, so that we take the responsibility ourselves. If we have ever been shafted in this regard it has been our own fault. We have opened ourselves, and somebody may have done us in either deliberately or by mistake; nonetheless it was our own fault because we weren't taking responsibility for ourselves, seeing what was going on, following through on our urgent concern for real values, spiritual values. I think there are many areas in all of us which need to open up so that a clarity may come. As I say, people tend to hold things back either because they want to keep a little something off on the side that they don't want anyone else to know about or maybe they're afraid to open up. But one way or another those things need to be released before what we really are inside can come through.

So the doors must be opened, and are when personal responsibility is assumed in the matter and we are bold enough to go where we need to go to open up and to begin to follow through the implications of that in our own particular experience. So all this weakness which tends to sit on top of the human heart may begin to dissipate and be gone. In that is maturing, and no matter how much we may learn, how proficient we may become in a thousand different ways, if this lump is still present on our hearts it's all to no avail; we get nowhere. We may go around saying how wonderful we are, and people may believe it. They may say, 'Well so-and-so is very proficient at this or that in the physical, mental or whatever way,' but it really means very little until that heart is opened, and until the current of life in all its clarity can move through to begin to channel this proficiency, or lack of it, in some kind of positive way, some way which actually fits with the grand design of life, which no one could figure out with their bright mind. The mind would be in that case a separate observer from what is really going on in life. Only as the heart opens do we understand and can the mind begin to be used in a way which is truly effective and useful.

I know, in my own experience along the way, that I have been most thankful for the fact that there were those with whom I could commune, with whom I could begin to open up and trust. As I say, not to lay myself on them but to allow them to provide a counterpoint for my own unfoldment. There is this need! I know that many have said to me along the way, 'Well, you had a special privilege; after all, you lived in the home of a spiritual leader for many years and whenever you had a question, whenever you wanted to open anything up with him, he was right there, no doubt, to give you the answer.' Let me let you in on something. He never told me anything! But there was a point of spiritual orientation which provided a base for me to take responsibility for myself, so that when the question was asked, genuinely asked, the answer could be given, not by someone else but by myself. If you're looking around for someone else to tell you the answer to the secrets of life, the mystery of the ages, what you should do tomorrow, or whatever, you haven't seen the point, because when you can genuinely ask a question, you already then have the capability of working out the answer for yourself. But it doesn't work out that way unless we are linked up with a counterpoint. There must be someone around to do that with. As I say, you can look up into the sky all you like, but nothing will really happen. It all tends to be a dream. However, everything is brought down to earth when there is somebody sitting right there you have to talk to. That is very much of the moment. We tend to avoid those moments sometimes because they probably will be quite uncomfortable. There are things down inside, squiggly-wigglies, that seem better left unsaid, untouched, that we fear might be too much to handle, that would leave us sick for a week. Well great, let's get it out. Welcome this kind of cathartic! How vital to maturity the matter of the open heart is. And it just comes along quite naturally provided we begin to open up in that way and to hold things steady when we do so.

I am most thankful personally — and I'm sure many of you feel that way too — for the consistency in spiritual expression which has been present over the years through our own leader. We know, in receiving a mailing which is the transcript of some talk he has given, that we can count on it being right on key. That's not to say that we shouldn't read it with a great deal of alertness. The tendency is, on the part of people — and this is what often produces reaction on the part of others looking on — just to go along gobbling up whatever is presented like a hog at the trough, with no intelligent listening at all. But thoughtful consideration, in a responsible way, of what is presented can begin to stimulate new comprehension of the truth. There is a tremendous need for that. As there is consistency in that kind of approach to things the light increasingly begins to come on. By reason of the consistency through this one particular man a cohesive body of many people has emerged throughout the world, not in any way because he went out and thumped a tub, but because he simply was himself and went through this process himself. And incidentally, back along the way he opened his heart very specifically in the direction of someone else who represented rightness. By reason of that action his spiritual maturity came, and then by reason of his consistency something more began to extend to others around him. But it is entirely secondary to what really matters, and that is the open heart in the direction of spiritual expression. That's the only thing of significance. If that is done everything else will fall into place.

Along the way I have thought, 'Here we are concerned with the development of spiritual expression in the world. Now how are we going to work that out? What should the plans be for this? How's it going to be put together? What kind of government will be involved? How's it all going to work itself through in a practical sense?' Too big for the little biscuit in my head to figure out! And yet, as the heart is kept open in the right direction then the form naturally unfolds. It has unfolded as far as it has, not because anyone manipulated; in fact if there has been manipulation it has stood in the way of the real outworking. People who have sought so much to help, and wanted to do this and that and maneuver this way and that, without opening their hearts, got in the way.

To trust, in the deepest sense of the word, that is the key! Unless there is that kind of openness all we have is a bunch of hardened concepts that may be shifted around and improved upon from time to time and it's all a big game, just like all the other games in our world which humanity has been playing for a long time. But when we begin really to open up in the innermost sense then something new can begin to appear, that is the real thing. The grand design of the universe as it relates to this place where we happen to be can begin to come through into experience, and we begin to understand what it's all about. There is something magnificent to be experienced in the way of life. What an adventure to let it happen!

A talk given to a group in Phoenix, Arizona, August 1976.

ALAN HAMMOND was born and educated in England, and came to North America in 1960. After several years of teaching from elementary schools to adult education and counseling in Canadian penitentiaries, he became a faculty member of the Emissary Servers Training Program in Loveland, Colorado.

During the past ten years Mr. Hammond has appeared on radio and television, and provided the focus for psychology, philosophy and holistic symposia throughout the country. He has assisted in coordinating communal patterns of living and provides a point of focus for the audiovisual programming in mass media for the Emissary Society.

MAN AS PRIMARY CAUSE

Alan Hammond

It is a great pleasure to be a part of the 'Whole Earth Days' symposium. It's such a tremendously large subject that one might think that in three days any group of speakers one wishes to gather together could hardly bring it to any kind of meaningful focus at all. And yet I think it is possible.

The brochure says, 'A forum for the consideration of planetary responsibility.' We all know that we're not the first to have that idea. There are universities, colleges and forums of all types who consider this subject. But it is emerging in the consciousness of the human race that something very new is required. The world has never been in quite the precarious position that it now is, and I don't have to take any of my time to elaborate upon the potential threats not only to human life but to the animal and vegetable life also on the surface of the planet. And yet, as far as I am concerned, I don't feel reason for pessimism. This is not a matter of 'Well I'm all right, Jack,' because, after all, I'm on the earth as well as everybody else. But fundamentally I trust life. Life, whatever it is, is very vast, and apparently it knows what it is doing. Somehow the human race has lost touch with this vast something or other that knows how things fit together in a living organism.

If we look through human history we find that in moments of crisis, at certain junctures in the history of man, there have been radical changes in the whole pattern of thought and feeling and behavior. The Renaissance is probably one example of such a juncture. But I feel that if ever there was a corner to be turned, now is the age when one needs to be turned. We are the ones alive now, and whatever corners are going to be turned must be turned by the people who are alive now. In these new developments in the history of mankind there was something which was at first indefinable. A previous speaker used the word *flow*, and you may have thought, 'Well what the dickens is a flow?' A flow of life. We're talking about something which is intangible and initially indescribable. A new spirit, a spirit of an age, one might call it. And after something which is indefinable begins to move through certain people, after that particular quality of feeling or new spirit has started to move, that new spirit produces new ways of looking at things, and people begin to live in a new way. But it is indefinable at first to the masses, to us. And yet there is change all the time in this living organism called the universe, called the earth. So from my point of view I feel we are living in extremely exciting times. The challenge is not to carry on in the old technological ways and hammer out refined present paths, because the paths we are now on are obviously leading to disaster. Like the last speaker, my interest is in people, because the primary factor, the primary cause on this earth insofar as the sentient life forms are concerned, is man. Human beings are forever moaning about their problems and yet the vast majority of their problems are caused by their own behavior.

Wars don't create themselves, people cause wars, people cause that problem. Pollution doesn't just drop out of the skies, people cause pollution. Poverty isn't caused actually by anything other than human self-centeredness and greed. If you really analyze the situation you will find that the problem lies in the distribution of resources. What about disease and other great problems confronting human beings? Human beings are supposed to be the poor, unfortunate victims of a hostile universe, threatened by things like germs, which are constantly giving us all these diseases. Well there are two parts to the answer, I would like to suggest. First of all it isn't a hostile universe or we wouldn't be alive. Whatever the vastness of life is, it conspired to bring us into these forms, to have this delightful, potentially exquisite experience of life. Think of all the billions of factors in the universe which come to focus on this planet to give rise to the life forms that are here, and we know it is potentially exquisite and delightful. The hell, the problems that I have outlined, exist because human beings are functioning in a way they need not function.

Disease is one such problem actually. It is known that the quality of emotion or quality of spirit that comes through human beings causes their diseases. I think psychosomatic medicine indicates that if you have destructive emotions – and by destructive I mean something like anger or resentment or jealousy or bitterness – if you have these qualities of character moving through you, you are liable to bring abnormal tensions into the body and you get diseased in various ways. The body isn't up to par, hasn't got the energy, is busy with conflict within itself, and the little bug that normally would be disposed of with a snap of the finger becomes something that causes trouble. That is a simplified presentation but that is the basic principle.

So all the human problems with which mankind is wrestling are caused by people, the way people behave. You can have United Nations, you can have legislation trying to keep the peace, you can have scientific discoveries that are trying to alleviate the ill effects that are proliferating in man's world, but the problem is not out there. It is like trying to sweep the ocean back with a broom to get rid of all these effects. The cause of the problems, the primary cause, is man himself and the way he functions, the quality of the spirit that is coming through him. If you have a destructive spirit emerging through man, a destructive quality of character, that destructive spirit takes form in the civilization which appears around man. Therefore it is more sensible to turn off the taps, if there is a flood in your house, than it is to spend all your time getting the bucket and sweeping up water. Why not go to the tap and deal with the source of the problem, which is the quality of character, the quality of spirit that is moving through man?

The 'Whole Earth Days' symposium, it says here, is 'a forum for the consideration of planetary responsibility.' Now, I've been to university and so have you, and you've heard so-called experts who theorize as to how the problems of the world in ecology, politics, science, medicine, could be solved if only man would follow out this or that pattern of political theory, scientific theory, psychological theory, sociological theory, religious theory, or what have you. It can be, and usually is, just hot air, because what about the ecology of the individual life? It is all very well to imagine that one has the solution for the world, and yet if the ecology of one's own little world, the ecology of a person's private world, is disrupted, if there is unfulfilment in various aspects, if there is chaos in such an expert's life, what does he know about harmony? What does he know about the true nature of life, true creativity, if his own life is filled with chaos, unhappiness and frustration? 'Well,' you may say, 'that is pretty unfair.' You may not see the correlation which I'm making here, but there is a very definite flaw present when a theorist, who can escape responsibility through his supposed solutions for the whole world, advises, 'Millions of people can be administered and brought into a harmonious state of relationship' – when his own life is a mess! It is idiocy. Until there are human beings who begin to assume, not planetary responsibilities, but personal responsibility for the order and beauty and nature of their own lives, they don't know what they are talking about. In fact all the problems of the macrocosmic civilization can be boiled right down to your own life. Your own world is a microcosm of the planet's problems, be it foreign affairs, finances or relationships. What tensions and frustrations are in your personal relationships? Have you got that area moving on a creative basis yet? Or are there still people you hate and dislike and all the rest of it? Because the seeds of international wars are in the individual lives, and so it is with all the problems I have mentioned.

So in the few minutes I have left I would like to outline to you how we can begin to assume personal responsibility so that the natural health, beauty, delight and fulfilment which are inherent in the design of life itself can begin to emerge in our personal lives, so that the design begins to appear somewhere on earth. If we have everybody pontificating in universities, governments and elsewhere about how it can all start but it doesn't actually start, we have a problem. And that is the problem, because people are either too afraid or discouraged to begin to assume personal responsibility for themselves to get into the flow of which we were speaking.

I'd like to provide an illustration. Here you are and here is your world around you. Now earlier I mentioned the very great impor-

tance of the spirit that is moving through a civilization. Boil that
down to yourself. And I wish to demonstrate to you that your
physical world around you, the circumstances of your life, the relationships you have, the financial situations, the job you have, all
these physical, environmental factors in the physical world are
brought there primarily by you. You are the primary cause of your
world. There are other causes, there are other influences, that is
true, because we are all part of one whole, our worlds overlap, but
you are at the center of your unique world. Nobody else is. You
are, and what is appearing around you is appearing there by reason
of the quality of something invisible that is constantly radiating
out of you. You can't stop life coming out of you. You can see some
physical substance here in my physical form, but what I'm beginning to point to is that there is something invisible coming out of
this form, radiating out of it, which is actually the powerful ele-

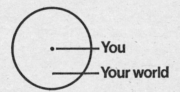

ment. The physical earth itself, the globe, moves through space,
moved by who knows what. Call it gravity, call it some force, but
there is something invisible which controls physical substance, and
there is something invisible which actually builds your world. And
this is important. By the way, in what I'm saying I'm talking about
civilization, yes, but primarily about your personal world. The
quality of your invisible spirit, the nature of it, the character of it,
is building your world, and I'll demonstrate how.

This life is what is coming out of you. You can't stop the stuff
radiating out, it just keeps coming. Even if you just sat there you
must realize that life is coming out. And this radiation is building
your world all the time; you can't prevent it. These are the laws of
life we are talking about and you can't circumvent them. But
supposing you express out through your mind and through your

body, we'll say, a destructive spirit. When I use the word *spirit* I'm not getting religious. I'm referring to the quality of spirit you express. Suppose it is a miserable, bitchy spirit – 'Damn university!' Now you can see that reflected by my contorted face here. I want to impress on you that this invisible something which is moving through me is already beginning to create and affect the physical world of my face. It begins to influence it and mold it according to its nature, immediately. Say 'To hell' with something or other. See what it has done to the physical aspect that is closest to me? I'm really angry about something! I'm resentful and I hate the government or the Communists, I hate the Republicans or somebody. Now you can see my distorted facial expression. Yes, it is amusing and it is simple, but it is very important. This invisible radiation of a certain spirit through you begins to change the physical substance of your world. It actually begins to change the substance of your consciousness also. If you feel angry, that current of feeling generates angry thoughts, that current of spirit moves out and begins to affect the physical body itself. If it is a destructive spirit it begins to have a destructive effect on the physical substance of your own body. Hatred causes abnormal tension, and so on. That tension, as I indicated before, may bring on disease, psychosomatic disease. The body then, with these abnormal, destructive energies moving through it, begins to disintegrate. It is destructive. So that spirit moves out past your body, which suffered as that particular current of spirit moved out from you, until it gets out into the environment beyond your body. You can see already, on a general basis, that if it is destroying all the way through the physical organs, it is going to continue to destroy any true design that life might be trying to create in your environment.

But specifically how does spirit build your world? Suppose you come into college or your place of work in the morning. You come into the classroom and you say, 'Damn the professor we have to listen to today! Who wants to hear him anyway? And did you hear what the president said? We have got to pay more fees. What a rotten system! Let's join the radicals and fight.' Obviously here is a certain spirit that you are radiating all around you. And people radiate an atmosphere, you can sense it, it is there. They are creating their world. But anyway, you are in the classroom or wherever, moaning, bellyaching away, expressing this destructive, miserable spirit, and someone may come over and say, 'You are damn right! We ought to do something about it, and furthermore he did this, that and the other rotten thing.' Now, do you see what you have done? In the expression of that particular quality of spirit you drew closer to you somebody who felt at home, who could harmonize with the quality of energy you were radiating. So you drew this person to you. You have begun to influence your physical world. You begin to draw to you those people who can harmonize with the quality of spirit you are giving out. Now, that person is also the center of a world, and if he is a habitual belly-acher, complainer, whiner, he has drawn in like manner others around him whom you haven't met yet, his friends, they are there. You haven't actually encountered them yet but you have not only drawn him closer to you, you have drawn his whole world closer to you. And if it has been primarily a destructive quality of spirit that he has been expressing those cronies will have destructive effects in their private lives also, their relationships will be full of conflict, disaster; maybe they can't handle money because they are either greedy or lazy or something or other. This is a very simple principle, and it is also vital, because you do build your world by reason of the quality of invisible spirit you express. Everybody does.

We as human beings have built the world, the civilization in which we live. And virtually nobody will assume responsibility for the state of society, and when it comes down to the individual, the individual won't assume responsibility for his own world. 'I'm un-happy. Why is my life such a mess? Because of my parents. My personal life is a mess because of the mess my parents were.' Oh yes, blame them! 'I've been unhealthy all my life. It is because of that. It is because of the other thing. It is because I haven't got enough money that I express this bitter spirit.' And we have a thousand excuses and reasons why we do not express our true, noble, creative quality of character. We even have excuses ready-made for us. 'We are born sinners.' That is a religious idea. 'We evolved, so we are animals.' That is another rationalization. 'Parents, society, have twisted me, so I have to be the stinker I am.' There are thousands of rationalizations a person will offer as to why he cannot express the true, noble qualities of character in absolutely every moment of living. Suppose you have a headache: 'Shut up! My head aches! You would be obnoxious like this too if you had a headache!' Actually it might clear up if you were not obnoxious. But anyway, people say, 'Shut up, I've got a bad headache.' And the idea is to convince other people that you have a reason for expressing a petty, self-centered quality of spirit and attitude. But you know, even if you manage to convince them, even if you fool yourself and everybody does believe you are miserable and sad and that you are justified – suppose everybody believes you, and you continue to express the miserable spirit because you have justified it to yourself and others – it doesn't change the effects of so doing. The laws of life keep on working. If you still express the rotten, miserable spirit, the law works and it keeps flowing into your body and world beyond, creating a greater hell. You haven't done anything except fool yourself, and that is what people do if they refuse to accept personal responsibility for the quality of character they express. The laws of life create around us according to the nature of the spirit we express.

It is true we may all have been damaged by our parents, we have been damaged by society, but somewhere there must be men and women who begin to grow up and not stay impotent, useless pawns of their environment. Man is the primary cause. If the world is going to have any radical changes in it it is because man changes, because I change. I must begin to identify with the quality of true character, a quality of spirit which, if I express it in every moment whether I feel like it or not, enhances a maturing process that one has to begin to move through. Where else is there to go? What else is worth doing? What could be more horrible than to have lived life and not fulfilled the inherent greatness of character which we all know is present within us? And if we don't deliver that, come what may, we will know that we were failures.

One great secret with which to conclude. We experience what we express. If you express a rotten spirit, that is the kind of experience you have right then. There is an idea that as you give, so you receive. People don't really believe that. But you know, you get it before anybody else gets it, because if you express a miserable, whining, sniveling spirit you get it, experience it, before anybody else gets it. You are giving it into the world, that's true, but you feel it and you experience the sniveling and whining character as you express it. What beautiful justice this is! So we can choose to have a totally different quality of experience. We can choose to express a noble, creative quality of character in every moment, no matter what the situation. You express that quality of spirit and you will find that that is what you experienced in that moment. You can't do otherwise, because that quality of spirit is moving down through your consciousness, through your experience. You experience what you express.

So if we wish to have a glorious earth – which we all at some time have sensed is possible – let us not look for humanity at large to do anything, because humanity at large isn't going to do anything, individuals are going to do something. You have your life to live. What is the quality of it – what is the quality of its expression? Because determining the quality of your experience is the quality of your expression. Let us experience the glory of life because we express the glory of its true character.

Talk given at a 'Whole Earth Days' symposium, York University, Toronto, Ontario, Canada, February 3, 1976.

FREEING THE MAGNIFICENT YOU

Alan Hammond

We all sense that there is something magnificent to express if only we could do it. It hasn't been done very often, obviously. We may think of the people we know, there aren't too many we would describe as magnificent. If we look into history there have been people magnificent in certain aspects of life, but who wants to be a genius at discovering machinery, shall we say, and yet be a complete flop as far as one's personal relationships are concerned? Surely what we are looking for, with everyone on the face of the earth, is the experience of fulfilment in every moment. I don't suppose many have achieved that, but just because we don't know many who have ever done it doesn't mean to say we couldn't have that experience ourselves.

So how is such a thing possible, even conceivable? I suspect if people really believed that they were magnificent this meeting room would be jammed with people. Most people think they are a bit of a mixture – 'I'm beautiful in some areas, but in others I'm pretty mediocre, if not utterly crummy, and I don't foresee much radical change. This may be a positive-thinking talk but I know basically that general approach.' So it would be very disheartening if that was all I was going to offer, it would be no better than anybody else had offered. I wouldn't bother to waste my time.

I think one thing we could assume is that if someone was experiencing their magnificent self as opposed to their crummy self, they would find themselves living in a magnificent world. It would be a magnificent experience, presumably. And that is the fact of the matter. Most people looking out on the kind of world they see and experience wouldn't describe it as magnificent. They would describe a world with its ups and downs, its blazing moments but also its sad moments. The truth is that it is a magnificent world; life is supposed to be a magnificent experience. If it isn't a magnificent experience the answer is not to dash hither and yon trying to get in on the magnificent action just as it breaks somewhere. That can be pretty exhausting, and you never quite catch up with the good times – have you noticed that? It is one big dash from club to club, from boudoir to boudoir, trying to get in on the magnificent times. Wouldn't it be much more satisfactory if you could produce magnificence wherever you are? Obviously it would be the answer, because it would save a lot of perspiration and dancing around, a lot of worry, wondering where to dash next in case you miss out on the big chance in life.

The key to it all is freeing the magnificent you, because when you free the magnificent you you find you are in a magnificent world. There are worlds within worlds. We say that there is only one world, the earth, and yet you could say there are as many worlds on it as there are people. Despite all our protestations of being humanitarian or altruistically minded, let's face it, it is your own world that you should be concerned about. All these people who are so worried about making everybody else happy are usually rather miserable because they are unable to make other people very happy, so they are not experiencing a magnificent world. The way to bring people into a magnificent world is not to try to convert them into it. Most people are experiencing a lie, they are not in the true world, they are in a kind of mirage world of misery. The way to allow people to come into the real world, the world that life designed us to have, is not by rushing around feeding people and somehow trying to persuade them to accept a long list of beliefs so that they will enter a magnificent world after they are dead. They are really going to live it up after they are dead! – which doesn't seem very sensible. Presumably, if life created us in this world it was to experience something tremendous here and now, to do something tremendous here and now, not to be hanging around afraid of living and therefore afraid of so-called dying. People who are afraid to die actually have been afraid to live. When you come to experience the truth of living everything changes and you are not concerned about, 'Will I be in heaven when I die?' because you are in heaven now. You are in this magnificent world now. The vast majority of people are obviously having a mediocre experience, therefore I know right away that they are not experiencing their true identity.

Who is a person's true identity? Who are you? Now, you may say, 'Joe Blow,' or whatever your name is. That is just a label your parents stuck on the form when you were born. That isn't you; that is just a name, after all. Who are you? Life, whatever that is, that colossal power, the only power there is, is expressing itself through all the forms of life that there are – through trees, flowers, birds; all these life forms have been created. Obviously life, this one power, is expressing itself through these forms. What else could it be? It must be that. Now what about this, my physical form? This is just a pile of atoms drawn up into this shape through which the one power of life is expressing itself. So the identity here isn't the bundle of atoms which has just been conveniently drawn up into a particular form. The identity is whatever it is that is expressing through the form. So actually you can't see me. You may have thought, 'Oh there he is,' but no, you haven't seen me yet, you've just seen this body through which I am expressing myself. You can't see me though I'm here all right. It is rather remarkable when you think about it. I have some equipment, I have this body, a mind with which to think, I have feelings and can express feelings through this emotional realm; so I have this equipment of body, mind and emotion. But that isn't me. I'm using all this equipment, so who is it talking to you? If I am able to express myself clearly through this form with no hang-ups, which may have been imposed upon it by its parents or by society, if this is a clear channel, who is talking to you? Life is! There is only one life, there is only one power. I mean, where else would we look for this identity? Who is doing all the action? Life! Life is who we are, individual aspects of life. That is the true identity.

Now, that is a very magnificent identity. We in our present experience of life may have thought ourselves to be little Joe Blow, American. Who are you? 'I'm an American.' No you're not! That's just where the body happened to take form on earth, and then it was stamped with the American label. You are not an

American, any more than trees are. Life isn't American, life isn't English, life isn't French, life isn't Chinese. Those are outer labels, which are very secondary to the true identity. People have been having such a mediocre, pathetic experience because they didn't even know who they were. In fact if you ask virtually anybody who they are they will give you the wrong answer. It is an incredible state of affairs; nobody knows who they are. However, all of that can be changed, and the very fact that you are at this meeting now is a part of your unfolding life experience.

A flower opens easily, very naturally, without any great sweat. You don't hear flowers moaning and groaning trying to be themselves. You do hear human beings moaning and groaning all the time: 'Life's so hard!' It is hard to be what you are not, that's why it is hard. If life is such a burden to people, so tough, it is because they are not being what they are supposed to be. If my eye tried to be an ear, really tried – it doesn't know how to, presumably – but if it really tried to be an ear, wouldn't that be a tiring, frustrating, futile business? But human beings are trying to be what they are not. They are trying to live up to images that were imposed on them by parents, society, the whole mass consciousness. We make up an image to live up to – if we're men, the hard-rock type maybe; or perhaps if we are ladies, the wilting violet or something. Think of your own image. It is disastrous. If you succeed in living up to that image you are going to be frustrated because you are already designed to be somebody, it is already all there. You didn't have to think very hard when you were a baby to decide how tall you were going to be, how many hairs you were going to grow, or the color of your eyes. The design was already there. What was the problem? There is no problem Human beings are busy making their own problems. Life has already designed everything. Why can't we just emerge into it and enjoy it! And we will enjoy it if we begin to be what we are designed to be, this true identity. I'm not going to paint some magnificent you and draw it in outlined dos and don'ts for you, because there is no need. I know it is already there.

Human beings have been so frustrated because they have been trying to be an ear when they were an eye, not trusting life at all.

People don't trust life, as though life doesn't know all about them! Yet if you look anywhere, you can't find anything that isn't designed. Your body is already meticulously designed to do a particular job, from your finger to any inside organ. Anything you look at in life is specifically designed to do a specific job, right down to the minute atom. Even atoms are designed. And in the vaster things, the biggest thing we can see, the cosmos, the universe, that is all designed too. And it works beautifully. Everything is designed it seems. Normally, we don't fret too much about our bodies working, they work very well. The sun rises in the morning – it is going to come up. But when it comes to our individual lives, 'Well now this is something really to worry about, to get organized here. I mean, I've got to map out my own life here.' What a stupid attitude! Don't we get a hint that maybe there is another way of doing things, not such a burden? People aren't straining to grow hair – well some are, they're getting a little thin on top! But in the course of events no one is straining to grow hair, it just comes. Now why can't the affairs of our lives work out the same way? Some people worry in case they are not going to get married; other people are worried because they did get married! But many people worry that they are not going to get married, we'll say, or find someone proper to live with. Well what a silly thing to worry about! Little birds don't neurotically drop their feathers because they haven't got enough sex appeal. Human beings do though. They worry. They think they've got hang-ups, and they have, but it is all such a stupid waste of time. Life has already designed all of our equipment. You're not going to be attractive to everybody (actually that would be a nasty mess if you were). No, there is a design to life. If you are exuding a phony self you are going to attract wrong people to you. That's what happens in the world, everybody is exuding a wrong self, so the wrong people are attracted and then they wonder why they don't get along. They are not supposed to be together in the design, that is why. It is so obvious.

The first job is to be oneself, discover something about that, and then there is no problem at all. You are just yourself in the design. Then whoever is attracted to that particular self can't help it any more than your fingernail can help being on the end of your finger. Where is the problem? There is no problem in true identity, that is how it all works. Life knows everything is all right. Life knows it is all designed. There is no worry if we are identified correctly. It is only people who aren't in their true identity that don't trust life, they think they have to make it all work and they make a big mess. Good! Let them suffer. If they are not going to be something magnificent, their true selves, the sooner they are eliminated the better, isn't that right? Wouldn't it be awful if misery continued eternally? Some people think so-called death is a bad thing, but can you imagine what it would be like if these distorted, bitter, twisted and disillusioned human beings went on living on and on and on? Wouldn't it be awful? Fortunately distorted things pass away, including distorted human beings. Now, you may not be able to agree with that point of view at the moment, but if you are identified with life you can. Life is eternal. The forms come and go but life doesn't die, and we begin to know this.

What about this true self? Who is going to start experiencing the true self? – because, as I said earlier, the fact that you are at this meeting means that there is something opening in your consciousness about yourself. The true way of life is being offered to you by life and it is all very easy. How many philosophy books have waffled on endlessly, waffled on about the mystery of life. 'Oh it is such a big mystery.' Well whoever thinks it is a mystery obviously never found the answer, so why bother to read their book if they don't know the answer? Why get lost with people who know only the problems? Oh people know the problem! Human beings are so unhappy. That word *unhappy* covers a multitude of problems, and social workers discuss social problems, psychiatrists discuss psychiatric problems, marriage counselors discuss marriage problems, and economists discuss poverty problems – problems, problems, problems. They are all discussing the problems. The only person to listen to is somebody who has found the answer. And to discover if they've found the answer don't just listen to their words. You need to have a closer examination of the state of their experience. You get philosophers waffling on, religious people waffling about their theories, about life, about God, about this, about that and the other thing, and they are miserable. What do they know about life? Their heads are just stuffed with ideas.

Last week a fellow came to Sunrise Ranch. He was a layabout if you ever saw one. He was at the Ranch for about four days, I think, and didn't lift a finger to help anywhere. He wanted to have a talk with me. He was droning on about cosmic consciousness, which had descended upon him in some mysterious experience or other while he sat cross-legged in the desert, and he figured that he was now in the midst of the Christ consciousness, the cosmic consciousness, and had touched the great masters. The fellow was a dreamer. His head was stuffed with stuff he had heard, that somebody had told him about. But that didn't mean anything insofar as experience goes. He was no good to himself and no good to anybody else either, just a self-centered sponge. And he thought he had cosmic consciousness! The nature of life is magnificent – not a lazy good-for-nothing, not a pathetic sponge!

So what I am getting at here is that the concepts you hear bandied around may be worth very little. They may be useful. Concepts, ideas, concepts briefly held, can be useful as signposts toward the truth. But the truth is an experience, it is the true experience of life. The truth is heavenly, the truth is magnificent, and if somebody is not having that experience don't bother to listen, they don't know. They will waffle on. They think they know something, they think they know the truth because they have this cosmology or that theology, but do they know the kingdom of heaven which is within and at hand, a heavenly experience possible here and now? Do they? If they do, well maybe they have something to offer, because the experience of heaven is what everybody on the face of the earth is looking for, even in a beer parlor! Everybody on the face of the earth is looking for the experience of heaven, the truth, the true experience, which they all sense should be magnificent. It is quite obvious though that most people are looking in the wrong place. There is nothing wrong with their looking – and they are all looking in different places – but who has found it? We find heaven now and then, don't we? We've all been in heaven, we've known it. We've had heavenly moments when life was wonderful: 'What problem? Who cares? Life's wonderful!' But how to know it every moment, there is the rub. Well it is very easy. There is no mystery about it. It doesn't take a thick book to tell us how to experience the magnificent world of heaven on earth, which we should all be experiencing.

It is an individual matter. I was speaking about this matter of identity. You know, it is very easy to get lost in a collective identity. We noted that: 'Oh we are Americans,' or whatever nationality you are, or if you are religiously inclined you may say, 'Well we are Catholics.' The identity is still false. We are not Catholics. 'We are Buddhists.' 'We are yogis.' It is very easy to get lost in a collective thing, you scramble in under a collective umbrella that promises something wonderful. 'We are Christians,' and you herd in under that and feel safer. But really, if you huddle in under any umbrella and adhere to their rules and regulations, you are not going to be your true self, because those rules and regulations will squeeze you into an image and likeness they approve of, whoever 'they' are. So the collective identity is very dangerous, even though people do it to feel secure. If they were actually experiencing themselves, their security, their fulfilment, wouldn't be dependent upon a collective identity. What is required is personal responsibility, which is what people don't want to accept. They want to be swept along with the crowd into the heavenly state. It can't be done that way. Association with people is all right, in fact very desirable, inevitable, but don't think for a moment that belonging to a group is going to do it for you, because it requires your individual responsibility to be yourself if you are going to experience yourself.

What is the nature of your true self? The nature of the true self is magnificent, it is honorable, it is noble, it is just, it is cheerful, it is creative, it is careful. All these characteristics are the nature of life. That is your true nature. You sense this and you'd love to be all those things but it seems so difficult. It seems difficult because, as I have indicated, various things have been imposed on top of you which have twisted the true design. What has been imposed on top causes conflict inside. The real you seeks to find freedom from the false pattern which has been imposed on top. Human beings experiencing this conflict say, 'This conflict is life!' That isn't life, that is a distortion of life. And that is what we have all experienced – this frustration, anger, jealousy and discouragement. It all derives from the false imposition. The answer obviously is the freeing of the real you, and the real you is this magnificent character that always does the very best it can, always expresses the greatest quality of spirit, in every circumstance. That is the real you.

Now, most human beings are not willing to entertain the possibility of ever doing that. 'That sounds far too difficult.' But it isn't. There are always so many excuses, aren't there, for not being a tremendous person in the moment, giving something of real value and quality in every moment. There is always some excuse as to why we can't do it, and we have to begin to see that they *are* excuses. Those are the things that are imprisoning us – our excuses. Freeing the magnificent self, freeing the magnificent you, is freeing you from your delusions, the hypnotic spell you are under, which convinces you that you've got any excuse for not expressing this tremendous character. You've been so hypnotized by your parents, your past experience – 'You're crummy, you're inadequate' – so that when somebody comes along and says you are not that, you say, 'Oh I am, he doesn't know me.' The point is that you don't know you. I know you but you don't know you! Here is the problem. Why not entertain the possibility? I know you. I know that you are an aspect of life, this magnificent one vast power, an individualized aspect of it. I know that. If you don't think you are magnificent you don't know you. I know you, and I know that you can come out of the prison that you feel you are in. You can come out of purgatory, or hell. This magnificent world is the only real world, and the way to come out is to begin to see that we haven't got any excuse for not expressing something noble, something of which we can really be proud in every moment.

By the way, there is absolutely no other way. If you are not going to do this, well frankly you might as well drop dead now, it will save you a lot of trouble. Problems. Oh you are going to have lots of problems, aren't you? Well you are if you don't do this. Start now. It doesn't take long to begin to get the feel of oneself.

What are some of the excuses? 'You don't know my family. My

mother and father messed me up. They were messed up.' And that's true enough. How many people here have parents who are magnificent expressions of life? Not many. There may be one or two, but not many. They were mainly neurotic, frustrated, afraid, and they passed that on to us, subconsciously. There is no use in blaming them. But the point is, do we have the excuse in our mind? 'Well I had a very bad home, so I turned out the creep I am,' or 'I didn't have a home at all' – even sadder. It may have been a great blessing that you didn't have a home. 'My father was a drunkard, he always kicked my mother! My brothers beat me. So I'm a creep. You can't expect anything of me because of what they did! I'm going to go right through life this miserable failure, because of what happened the first ten, fifteen years of life.' What a pathetic attitude that is! Or, 'I'm going to whine and snivel through life, bellyache and bleed all over the place, because of what was done to me.' Isn't it pathetic? What a fine example of manhood and womanhood! 'I'm going to cry for the rest of my life because my parents were so cruel to me.' Poor you. A swift kick in the slats might do something! Or, 'I've a weak heart, I have a certain illness you know, so nothing very great can be expected of me. If any pressure comes on, oh my heart.' Always an excuse to do very little, always an excuse to moan and get people to do the most they can for me because I am so fragile. Anybody have a mother like that?

What other excuses are there? 'Oh I didn't have a very good education, I'm not very clever. I can't do anything in the world because I'm not very bright. The future is pretty dim for me, so I'm miserable and unhappy.' What a useless attitude! Success in life isn't dependent upon any of those external factors at all, it depends upon the quality of character you express in each situation. 'Well I can't really live now. I'd love to start expressing this wonderful character, I'd love to stop whining and complaining and moaning and criticizing everybody else, but I've got *this*. I'm still living at home and my parents bug me, so of course I've got to be pathetic because they are bugging me.' Or, 'I'm in this job, a very lowly job. The boss is terrible, these people all around me are terrible, so of course I've got to cry and snivel and complain and

cheat and twist because of this.' And if you say 'because of this'
. . . grow up! 'I can't express this tremendous character of life, I
can't offer something tremendous, because of this.' Well that 'of
this' is an excuse, it is a lie, it is letting yourself kill yourself, you
are imprisoning yourself, with an excuse.

You can express this great quality of character. You can express
greatness even washing the dishes. How many people when they
wash dishes whine about doing it – 'Oh what a drudge here!' –
instead of offering something of great spirit into it. You can be
great washing the dishes because you have this sense of greatness –
'I'm going to do these dishes as well as I can' – and take a pride in
washing the dishes, sweeping the floor. If you take a pride in every
single thing you do you will find yourself in heaven right away,
because the secret is that you experience what you express, you
experience what you give. If you are in hell or purgatory it is because you have been giving a stinking, mediocre spirit, but as soon
as you start taking a pride in the quality of character that you are
expressing in every situation, so that you do it as artistically and
as effectively as you can, you are in heaven – bingo! Just like that!

Now who would believe it was so simple? But that is the answer,
the expression of the magnificent you in every moment. You
express as magnificently as you can. It may not be a supernova,
and yet the experience is super, even in the smallest task. Most
people, when they think of a magnificent you, see a sunset and
themselves on top of the mountain with a flag – the magnificent
them – and a million people below watching their performance.
Well obviously, given a moment's thought, it is not likely to work
out like that, but we can still have a magnificent experience in
every moment. There is never a situation where there is any reason
to complain about anything, even though the factors involved in
the situation may be difficult. You, listening to me now, may say,
'Well I'm damned uncomfortable here. I've got a boil on my backside and I have to sit here and listen to this guy. How can I have a
magnificent experience?' Well you can, actually. You may be
aware of the boil on your backside which may be painful, but
nevertheless, moving in the spirit of what I am saying, you may
know victory. It is not that all discomfort is going to be removed

from your world or that difficult situations won't come up. Your mother may be an invalid in bed and you are living at home, etc. – I'm just trying to think up some hypothetical situations. That may not be the most wonderful situation seemingly, but nevertheless the expression of this true character pervades the whole experience and is magnificent in its totality. So there may be a few sticky elements present but the total experience is magnificent because you are giving expression to this magnificent spirit. Isn't this something, to know the answer of life at such an early age! It wouldn't matter if you listened to every philosophy on the face of the earth, listened to every religion, I have told you the essence of them all right here and now. This is the essence, the expression of this magnificent spirit, this character, which is the character of life, the character of God – God, or life, expressing through human form. Now, when you begin to express this spirit and this character which you are, who are you? You are an expression of being, of life, of God, whatever you call it. Let's not get hung up on a word.

So there is the answer – all in an hour. And you will never hear the answer much clearer anywhere, because unless whoever tells you anything tells you this they are wrong. This is the answer. And you can prove me right or wrong. I don't ask you to 'believe' in it. Do it and find out for yourself. But wouldn't it be awful, really, having heard the answer so clearly expressed . . . life speaking to you – not wandering through the woods and hoping to commune with nature, or God, through flowers and the trees. Well it is very nice to commune with the flowers and the trees but they can't talk to you as directly as life can speak to you through human lips. The answer can come very clearly through human form. And the answer is, 'Express the divine character, the true character of life, the quality of life, and you will be in heaven.' God is in heaven, so if you express the divine character where will you be? If you are the divine character where are you? In heaven! Human beings are in a mirage world. The truth is right with them, they are the truth in reality. And when we express our true selves the truth begins to appear all around us. It is like waking up. And that is what you are doing now, you are waking up to the truth of life, the truth of yourself. It is quite an adventure. There is no great struggle, providing we sense the colossal adventure that being alive is. And the wonderful experience which you think you should have in life you do have. You should have that experience, it should be magnificent. So why not have it?

It is worth looking into a bit, isn't it? Wouldn't it be rather remarkable if – of all the billions upon billions of human beings that have lived and died looking for the truth and never finding it – if you actually found the truth that they were all looking for? It is right with us. We weren't born to wander around wondering what life is all about. Wouldn't that be rather a waste of time? So let's not waste a moment, let's not waste any more time. Let's begin to be true to that magnificent character which we know is within us. It may have been buried, but begin to be true to it. And in being true to that you will emerge into the true experience of heaven on earth. Magnificent!

A talk given at Colorado State University, Fort Collins, Colorado, October 24, 1972.

BEING AT THE SOURCE

Alan Hammond

The earth is a living organism. And there are so many parts to this
planet, for example all the different kinds of flowers, foliage, animals, birds, fish, bugs – millions of them! What variety, all going
to compose this living organism called planet Earth. And we find
ourselves also alive, not just living on the planet but an integral
part of it, part of a living organism. Human beings haven't
thought of themselves as a part of a living organism. They have
thought of themselves perhaps as being on it, and yet if we were
in space looking at this planet, knowing all the forms of life there
are on it, we would recognize that whatever is on it is part of it,
it's one thing. Just as you might look at my individual physical
body here. There are different parts of it – hair, eyes, fingers,
hands. And that's just the outside, there are all the parts and the
organs inside, all are parts of a physical form through which life
expresses itself.

Within this form that you see here is an identity. Have you
ever thought perhaps that the earth itself has an identity? We
think we have individual identity, and of course we do, and yet
we're part of something greater, an entity which is greater. Isn't
it true that here is my finger, the identity of this form here is my
finger? Here is my thumbnail. These are parts of me, but the
identity of this form is within the whole structure and I express
myself through all the parts, to do what I wish to do. Is it not
likely that this planet has an actual identity of its own? It obviously has. We're just, as it were, an organ in the body of the living
earth. It has an identity. We as individuals can't encompass that
identity any more than the consciousness of my finger can encompass the whole identity of which it is a part; but it does have a

consciousness. Each organ has a consciousness, in order to play its part in the whole. And so it is with this planet. It has an individual identity in the family of the planets, in the solar system. But we are really interested, obviously, in coming down to earth and playing our part where we are. I'm seeking to open up perhaps a new way of seeing our setting and seeing what it is of which we are a part.

As we look around at the other forms in this body of the planet Earth, we may discover something very interesting with respect to the human spirit. We find that every other life form somehow reflects a part of ourselves. If you want to describe the eyes of a woman, you might say, 'Her eyes are exquisite, like stars.' Or if we like the complexion of her cheeks we say, 'They're like rose petals.' If we see a man who is particularly courageous and strong we say he's just like a lion. In this manner we describe aspects of the spirit coming through human beings at any given moment. You've seen people who are exactly like butterflies, you watch them flit along, expressing an aspect of the earth's spirit which is more particularly brought to focus in a butterfly. Anyway, at certain times human beings express the spirit which is, in its multitudinous manifestations, being expressed throughout the whole planet. In other words we find in human beings, in the human form as part of the earth's planet body, the apex of the planetary organism. We can express all the spirits made manifest through all the life forms. People can imitate trees. They can stand there and wave their branches and reveal the lithesome spirit of a tree, or a bird, or an animal of any kind, because the spirit of the earth comes to focus in man.

If the planet has an identity of its own it's much larger than human beings. Don't you think if we, as little parts of that identity, can express love, that the larger identity expresses somehow a greater love, a greater feeling? Don't you think it has a greater consciousness than we have, we who are a little part of the whole body? I suspect so. What about the intelligence of human beings? We have intelligence as part of this much larger form. Don't you think the total intelligence of the planet Earth is greater than the intelligence of man, which is a little organ within that body? We were considering how all the life forms have their own consciousnesses in order to play their parts. Well, what is the part of man then? What is really unique about mankind among all the life forms? There are many distinctions, but surely he is the apex.

At the physical level, the mental level, the emotional level, man has the ability to know himself, to have a conscious awareness of identity. If what I'm saying is true, if there is one energy, one power, one identity, which resides within this planet, through whom would that planet speak to express many things which cannot be expressed through any other life form – the nobility, the beauty, the grace, the delight, the joy, the majesty, of this character? Surely all those magnificent characteristics should come to their most eloquent expression through the human form embodying what we have called the human spirit, which is part of something much greater.

I'd like to read a poem to you which I think develops this line of thought. It is entitled 'The Eternal Presence.'

This planet's life I am,
Speaking through this little form into the realm of humankind.
Ho, little people who read these words,
Know ye not the One with whom ye speak?
I am He larger than any man,
Larger than all parts and capacities of everything upon this
world,
For I am the One whose body this earth is,
This planet's life I am.

Before man was, I am.
In every moment, every place,
Through the days and settlements of man,
I was.
Present was I in human form,
Witness of every event, both so-called mighty
And those completely unrecorded, unremembered, now
unknown.

No human thought, or feeling, aspiration, sorrow,
No plan or action, whether large or small, was made outside
                                                    My presence,

For I experienced all.
Before man was, I am.
When man is gone, I am.

This word, now uttered through this form,
Will pass anon.
Posterity does not need immortal words
For I shall speak what's necessary then.
But in this present moment of My experience
I utter words of love and life and joy.
This is a wondrous time, a wondrous place;
But on time moves, all outer clothing changes –
And I shall be present loving, living, thrilling
Then, as now.
If any read these words I spake,
Remember you wrote them then
As now you read!
For we are one, eternally.

This planet's life, I am.

I think that if you are willing to move with the spirit that is
offered here we begin to find an expansion in feeling, not intellectual concept merely. Are we all willing to let our true identity
appear? Human beings get bogged down in false identities, people
looking for themselves all over the place. People are frustrated
because they never do discover themselves, they never express
themselves fully in life. What are some of the false identities? I'd
like briefly to run through some in case you're hung up in any
of them, because you are not who you have thought yourself to be.

How many people get involved in roles that they play? 'I'm a
scientist, I'm a doctor, I'm a teacher, I'm a gardener, I'm a house-
wife,' whatever. That's not who any of us are. We may play
these roles but it isn't who we are. Other people tend to get

identified in their physical body. You're not your physical body. You have a physical body but you are not your physical body. If you hurt your arm you say, 'I've hurt my arm. My arm hurts.' It's part of your equipment through which you can express yourself, whoever you really are. You're inside this body somewhere, you are not your body. Other people tend to identify with their intellects. 'I'm my mind.' You're not your mind. Some people have very good minds, other people have pretty slow minds, and we have to work with them, whichever we have. But you're not your mind. You have a mind, it's part of your equipment through which to express yourself, but you're not your mind.

Many other people identify with their feelings. 'Oh I'm my feelings. I'm sad, I'm happy.' No, you're not your feelings. You have a capacity of perception and expression through which you can express feeling, but you are not your feelings. I can use my feelings to express something gentle, soft and delicate, or I can use my feelings to express something more powerful and strong. My feelings are merely a part of my equipment. So who am I? I'm not any of this outer equipment. Now, I'm going to say, 'I am life. I'm the energy that's expressing through the equipment.' This is just an idea to many of you but at least it's an idea which points in the right direction. Realization is not going to come all in a flash. We're changing direction, becoming aware of something vaster, discovering who we really are. Perhaps we can see now who we're not. But the question is, Who are we? Well obviously we are life, whatever life is.

The invisible power that is expressing itself through all life forms, that same one and only power is also expressing itself through this pile of dirt – the physical body – just a pile of dirt which life drew up into this form through which to express itself. And we are an aspect of that one power. It's undeniable. Nobody can deny what I'm saying, because it's so obvious. You think that you have sat there looking at me. But you haven't seen me actually; all you've seen is this pile of dirt through which I'm expressing myself! Isn't that something? Nobody has ever seen us. They've just seen our outer clothing which is our physical body!

Our true identity is this one power called life, expressing its glorious spirit, its creativity. That's the true nature of us all. It's a glorious character, a creative character. Yet people have other kinds of experiences, such as misery, frustration and unhappiness. People think that's the natural state. It isn't the real self, it isn't the natural state. This false state exists because the real you, the true design of you, as soon as you were born was covered over by a false design placed over you by parents, society, man as he now is, and that incarceration was established and instead of the real self being able to blossom and open up there was the false design over the top. And so we have these feelings of conflict, the feeling of imprisonment, then the feelings of anger and resentment experienced within people everywhere. Why? Because it's the natural thing? No! Because you've been incarcerated in a false identity. This is not the natural state that life intended. It is the state that everybody experiences but it is not the truth of your being.

And so we let the real character begin to emerge, the real self, the character of life, the creator, always creating in every situation, no matter how difficult. Let's look, for example, at a tomato plant planted in poor soil. Life doesn't bring the plant out through the soil and then say, 'To hell with it. I'm not going to bother to try, there's no good soil here, hardly any rain. I'm not going to bother to grow. I'll just let it stay as a seedling!' No, life makes the very best of the situation exactly the way it is. It has a creative attitude. That is the attitude of life, always creative, in every circumstance. Its character, its spirit, pours forth and makes the best of the situation. And that is *our* character actually. So our true identity is life itself. How marvelous it is to let our identity begin to change from the false identities, the mixed-up identity which we have thought ourselves to be, and to let a genuine experience of ourselves begin to unfold naturally.

A baby has a baby's consciousness of itself. You remember when you were a little child, you had the awareness that you were a child. Then you grew up into an adolescent and the sense of identity began to change. You were a bigger person. As you grew into adulthood you found that you'd left the adolescent sense of identity, sense of self, behind and you had a sense of being an even bigger person. Most human beings never get beyond that. They never grow into the fulness of their identity as an individual, as part of the planet and beyond. Let's not worry about that, but let's begin to have an expansive openness to the adventure of the unfolding experience of Self.

So it's a gradual process. By the way, nobody shoots from an infant to an adult in a flash. That would be awful! It's not the way life does things. We begin to yield to the true character of life, expressing it so that the true character is moving through us. You know, people try to grasp in order to enlarge their consciousness. They want to get 'cosmic' consciousness and they're reading books and worrying in case they don't discover everything and so on. Whereas the consciousness you should have is already built in. If you'll just begin to relax and open yourself to life, trust life! Begin to associate with those people who exemplify this quality of character. You love that quality of character, you express it. The spirit of life is moving through you and your own consciousness will begin to unfold just like any cabbage plant! For its design is already built in and we'll know what we need to know for what we need to do right now.

Most people think they are going to acquire a lot of knowledge and then they'll be able to know everything there is to know in the cosmos. Only an insecure person wants to do that, only somebody in false identity wants to do that, because all we need to know is what we need to know in the moment to do what we need to do in the moment as our part in the vast design. And that's very little actually. It is merely to express the right character, the right spirit in this and every moment. It's all much simpler than theologians, philosophers, psychologists, economists and scientists, and all other experts in their individual compartments have led us to believe. 'It's a hopeless task to understand life,' they say. But it all begins to be very simple as our identity moves back into the true quality of character, that noble, sublime character which we all sense we are here to express. When we begin to do it everything else in our-

selves, in our consciousness and in our worlds, begins to fall naturally into place. That is the simple truth. We are here to be
ourselves, to play our part in the design of life.

How privileged I feel to have been a part of this particular
'Whole Earth Days' conference, to participate in something that
is unfolding on earth – not an intellectual dogma or theology or
something being planted on everybody, no need, because everybody is already connected with life, you're already connected to
the source, the source is already within you. The source is life,
and your true identity is life. We may not be very consciously
aware of it today but if we increasingly yield to the character of
the source, life, we begin to find we are there at the source. We are
there. In fact we are here, life is present now, the supreme intelligence is here now. It's not somewhere else, we're part of it,
fundamentally. 'I am here.' This is our true identity – 'I am
being.'

So whole people are part of a whole planet, part of a whole
solar system, part of a whole galaxy, part of the whole universe.
Actually, if you trace this energy that is speaking to you now all
the way back, it is one character speaking, it is one identity speaking. That's not egomania. It's the truth. It's the obvious, undeniable truth. And we are part of that character. So what a
tremendous adventure it is to be in human form, to express
ourselves through the human form with all its multitude of
capacities, to express beauty and delight and joy, to express this
character which I am and you are.

A talk given at the 'Whole Earth Days' symposium, York University, Toronto, Ontario, Canada, February 1976.

GEORGE EMERY is a graduate of the University of Maine and Boston University School of Theology. For many years he was a Methodist minister, offering leadership particularly to those who were 'disenchanted' with the failure of traditional Christianity to meet their needs of spiritual fulfilment. More recently, he has been concerned to live and teach the way of life exemplified at Sunrise Ranch, headquarters of the Society of Emissaries.

Mr. Emery and his wife Joelle travel throughout the world, lecturing in colleges and universities, giving weekend and one-week Art of Living seminars, to provide a point of inspiration and orientation for those who desire to express their total potential in daily living.

A BALANCED PERSON IN A BALANCED WORLD

George Emery

I've been thinking about questions that people ask and how important they are. I have often said that if you don't ask the right question you never get the right answer. And some of those questions are very obvious, like 'Will you marry me?' That's a pretty important question. Or 'Do you think this is a good stock to buy?' But sometimes other questions that don't seem so obviously important may be just as significant, like the question 'Where will you be in March and is it possible for me to come and visit you?'

Now that doesn't seem like a very profound question, but I asked it seven years ago and it made all the difference in the world. I said to a man named Anthony Brooke, from Scotland, in December 1969, 'Where will you be in March and can I come visit you?' And he said, 'George, I will be at Sunrise Ranch, in Eden Valley, Loveland, Colorado.' And I said, 'Ah, come on. There isn't a place that exists in the world with an address like that!' He said, 'I've got a sneaking suspicion that these are real people. At least, I'm going to spend a month there to find out.' And in the middle of March he called me on the phone and said, 'Come on; the highest expression of truth I've ever seen is in Loveland, Colorado.' So we came, and it was the most meaningful experience of my life. It was the most significant experience of my life because I discovered my own significance. And when you really discover your significance and look forward to giving that significance in any moment, then any event is a significant event. So my life took a whole new surge, because I sensed something about a group of people living out in the foothills of the Rockies.

I've always had this sensing that if life was to be meaningful for me it would be meaningful because of people who could touch me and bless me and somehow draw from me that which I knew was present. Everybody had been telling me that I had great potential but so few people knew how to draw it forth. When I touched that group of people I began to discover something more of what that potential was.

There is another dimension that man can get in touch with, that in reality man, woman, rightly is, and that other dimension sees so-called problems, for instance, not as problems but as creative voids to be filled by the energy, the truth, of man. I touched many things along the way, and if I were to tell you all of them it would take an age. Many things, groups, people touched me and I was very blessed by them. But I always found, whether it was Eastern religions or Western religions or Transcendental Meditation or Joel Goldsmith or New Thought Alliance, or you name it – I've touched everything I could think of as I came along, because I had a deep desire to be everything that I could possibly be so that I could get on with doing what I came into the earth to do – yet everywhere I went I found myself quickly filling the particular box, the particular approach, with my energy, and thus finding that the ceiling would come off and the walls would come down, and I would walk on. But when I touched Sunrise I felt something different and I decided to give myself to this approach, this program, this way of life, and I did. And after seven years I see no hint of a ceiling and no sign of a wall! And that's what it's all about!

I took an article out of the *Denver Post* recently. It's written by R. Dale Liechty, a member of the staff at the University of Colorado Medical Center in Denver, and it's entitled 'What Are We – Homo Sapiens or Homo Faber?' *Homo sapiens* is supposed to be man the wise; *homo faber*, man the technician. It is an interesting article and I would like to read to you two paragraphs:

> Arnold Toynbee, the great historian, describes the same phenomenon as a metaphorical 'morality gap.' 'There is a great inequality of man's giftedness for science and technology on the one hand and religion and sociality on the other. And

this is to my mind one of man's chief discords, misfortunes and dangers. Human nature is out of balance.'

It always has been. And then this statement:

Few of us would argue against Toynbee's contention that human nature is 'out of balance.' In the play, *Butterflies Are Free*, the wise mother asked the visiting mod playwright why he felt it necessary to emphasize four-letter words. He glibly answered that it is simply 'part of life.' Her cryptic reply, 'So is diarrhea,' brought a thundering ovation.

Those who look upon the *Tao* as merely quaint or perhaps magical nonsense, who reject it absolutely, can expect, if their views prosper, that future Watergate conspirators, Hitlers, Mansons, or perhaps even worse, will reappear in other guises. But let's reject that gloomy vision. Man is, after all, *homo sapiens* (man the wise); – not *homo faber* (man the technician). Perhaps there are still enough philosophers – both professional and amateur – to reaffirm our *real* name and thus restore the balance.

Everywhere people are saying, 'Man is out of balance, the world is out of balance. What are we going to do?' Well you can reaffirm until the cows come home that man is *homo sapiens*, man the wise; you can affirm that man is this and man is that and man is everything. You can sit in the lotus position and affirm him. But unless you get up out of the lotus position and *express* man the wise, woman the wise, mankind isn't going to be restored to a state of balance nor is the world going to be a world of balance.

Man was created to be a balanced, wise person. And a good definition of wisdom is 'a sense of the fitness of things.' A wise man is the man who knows from his balanced position what is that fitting, appropriate thing to think, say and do in the moment, and then *does* it, for the good of the whole.

How does one become this, not only in theory but in actuality? How does the balanced man, the balanced woman, become actualized so that the balanced world can become a reality and not just a dream? I hinted at this when I said I found people who are more balanced than myself. These people were always saying to me, 'Let me accept you just as you are. And yet let me suggest to you that there is more to you than surgeons can remove; there's more.' And somehow they knew how to draw that forth from me. Charlie Brown said, 'The worst thing anybody can say to me is, "Charlie Brown, you've got great potential." '

I'd like to suggest that this human potential movement, which can be a tremendous stepping stone to balance for an individual in the world, can also be a terrible stumbling block. And there have been people in the human potential movement for twenty thousand years, parents who have tried to get their children to be something more, often so they could live their lives over again through their children. And by doing this they were actually dooming their children to a life of guilt and shame; in fact there were sixty-five million Valium prescriptions this last year, to help people with anxiety – millions of people with anxiety, a disease where the doctor doesn't know why the person is anxious, he's just anxious. Yet I would like to suggest to you that in my counseling over the years and my study of people, working with people, I've come to the conclusion that in the vast majority of the people who are anxious and don't know why, there is a subconscious sense of shame and guilt because they have not actualized the potential that is present. So they find themselves in their twenties, thirties, forties, not being what somebody else wanted them to be, much less who they really are, and then feeling very shameful and guilty about it and not knowing why. And then often people commit suicide, spending the rest of their life committing it on the instalment plan, or immediate suicide, because they do not want to face the fact that they are not fulfilling their potential, the purpose that they came into the earth to fulfil. So what do we do? People beginning to fulfil their potential, discovering their totality, discover an experience of balance and contribute to a balanced world. So let's take a look at what it might mean to be a balanced person in a balanced world.

Most people consider themselves maybe two-dimensional. In fact there are still people that, when you ask who they are, say,

'What do you mean? You're looking at me.' In other words they are so involved with their physicalness that they think that is all they are. Now there are sophisticated ways to cover that up, but when you talk to them about what is most important they have little ways of cluing you in – 'The most important thing is your health,' or 'Lips that touch inorganic foods will never touch mine.' They are into all kinds of things that show that the body is the most important thing to them.

And then, of course, there are others who will say, 'No, it is really not the body; it is the mind; mind over matter, this is the important thing. When the mind is filled with all the right programing and all the wrong programing is cleared, then that brings a balanced person.' May I suggest to you that the mind is not equipped to do that, because the mind is the *result*. What is in the mind, the conscious and subconscious mind, is the result of programing by out-of-balance people living in an out-of-balance world. And you may be programed with better concepts and better beliefs and better feelings and better experiences than you got out of your parent tape and child tape, but if you're still looking to something outside you, you are asking for a better imbalanced condition but it is still going to be imbalanced. The mind, anyone's mind, which is the result of external programing, is never the initiator of a balanced mind and a balanced body, because those are the two things that you *have*, but they ain't what you *is*. And only 'what you is' is going to bring you into an experience of balance.

But most people think that this is human nature. 'I am a result of my heredity, plus my environment, plus my reactions to my heredity and environment.' And so the pendulum swings from one end of the human nature spectrum to the other and we have over here the material approach and over here the spiritual approach. Many people think, because we've gotten everything we've wanted in the material line and it still doesn't bring us a sense of fulfilment, purpose, that we must go to the other end of the spectrum. So we've got all kinds of spiritual people who are no earthly good because they are so far over on that end of the spectrum. There must be a balance point somewhere between the two. Then there are those living in the mental realm and those living from the emotional realm, and of course those living in the past and those living in the future. People are constantly looking to another time or to the way things used to be, or to the future: 'I'll be happy when I get this or that.'

And of course we have people with what I call a 'billiard ball syndrome.' You know what that is? From the time you get up in the morning things push you around – the circumstance, the wife, the toast, the weather, whatever. How many people have no sense of direction because of this wishy-washy nature, controlled by externals. Then on the other side are the people who have set goals: 'I know exactly what I want and how I'm going to get it. I've got it all set up in a five-year plan.' And they get what they want, they get what they want. Then they find out it is not what they need; it is not really a blessing to themselves or to others.

So what is the answer? The answer is the possibility that there is more to you than this, which you will never know if you are living in any extreme of the human nature spectrum. It is only when you begin to be more balanced that you begin to discover that there is a third dimension, and a fourth and a fifth, sixth, seventh dimension, and behind this a tremendous totality!

Can you imagine people living out of two dimensions because of all these things that have been programed into them? They have little idea of what the third dimension is, or the fourth or fifth or sixth, because they live on one end of the spectrum or the other, where everything else is obscured. And the only way one really comes to discover one's totality and experience real balance and contribute to a balanced world is to move out of this 'billiard-ball syndrome' or 'set-goal syndrome' to a sense that there is a design, and one doesn't live in either the past or future but in the *now*. And when one begins to experience what that means and is not interested in the physical or mental or emotional approach but is aware of something more, there begins to be a different capacity other than these three familiar ones, and that capacity has something to do with knowing, because one deeply wants to know – not what is good or bad but what is right and fitting to think and say and do in the particular moment that one finds oneself in.

How deep is that hunger to know what is appropriate and fitting in a moment and then to express it, to know what is the attitude, the spirit, that is just right to express? It is that beginning sense of not being involved in the mental or emotional capacity but a sensing that there is another capacity, a capacity to know that right spirit, to discern it and to express it. Spiritual expression: the capacity to discern, to know in the moment; not dependent upon that which has been programed out of the past, not concerned about what is coming out of the future, but having a sense that, transcending the conditioned self, there is another self, another dimension. And when one deeply desires to know that, so that one can express out of that self what is appropriate, then one comes to know what one needs to know, say what one needs to say, and do what one needs to do, when he needs to know, say and do it.

But it takes hunger, a desire, a real gut-level concern about being right, and then expressing that; not sitting on it, not contemplating it, not writing books about it, but actually *expressing* it. You are what you express. And you only know what you are; you only know what you express. It isn't a matter of affirming that there are great qualities present, great potential. You can affirm these and meditate about them all you like but until you *express* them because of your deep desire to know what is appropriate and fitting these qualities are imaginary; they are not known until they are expressed. And when they are expressed one has a sensing of this very important fourth dimension, and it is here that we rightly dwell. I am that which I express. I do not express that which comes up out of my conditioning. I may *feel* anger, shame, guilt, but that doesn't mean I need to express it. There is an alternative. I can sense those things, those thoughts, those feelings, that have come from external conditioning, the results of all kinds of things coming on me from all kinds of places. But that is not what I am; it is what I have. What I am is love and truth and life; it is unconditional! That's what I am! And when I express it I know what I express. I am life, and I'm truth, and I'm love. That's the truth of me, because I know it, because I express it.

And when I express it I find myself at a crossover point between those invisible qualities and my physical capacities. And these qualities come into my earth, through me, blessing the body and the mind, blessing the world. It is not a matter of mind over matter; it is a matter of spirit over both. And I express the spirit of life! And I *love* to express the spirit of life; I just love to! Why? Because that is what I am and I love to be what I am, to express that which is true, that which is loving, that which is fitting, that which is appropriate. I love to because I was created in the image and likeness of spirit. And when I am doing that I am at that balance point. I find a balanced experience and I am beginning to contribute to a balanced world. And it is fun, easy, a blast!

What would you call this dimension? What would be a good word for that? How about the 'overworld'? Would that be a good way to say it? Would you be upset if I were to tell you that you have been living in the underworld all your life? Have you ever heard somebody say, 'That person isn't living up to his potential. He's got so much more to give. It's a crime!' Have you ever heard that? 'It's a crime!' Anybody who is living in the underworld, only knowing two dimensions, is a criminal. Now there are various degrees of criminality, but it is a crime to live in the underworld, to live under the vibrations, the thoughts, the beliefs, the concepts, the structures, that come as the result of trying to be at one end of the spectrum or the other. You know, the best thing one can ever do is kick our conscience out the window. Conscience is learned behavior; it is what somebody else taught you is good or bad; and it is never the appropriate thing, never. All kinds of good people have been doing good things and the world is in a mess!

Good people never can do the right thing, did you know that? Good people never do the right thing. It may be the *good* thing, but it is never the *right* thing. Only a right person, a person who knows his right, true identity, a person who is living in the overworld, living out of the unconditional quality, discerning that spirit that needs to be discerned, that word that needs to be said, that act that needs to be expressed, could ever possibly do the right thing. And the world is out of balance because of good people who are doing their best, but their best isn't enough because they are living in the underworld. They have got to come up to the overworld, so that the things of the overworld can come into the underworld and then the underworld is blessed and transformed and regenerated and resurrected and restored to its true position so that the over-world and the underworld are one. How do you like *them* words?

Buddha said to stop being identified with material things, to let go of those things, because what gets your attention gets you. And if you give your attention to the externals, the externals are going to control you and that is not where the control should be. He was no dummy, Buddha. Krishna had some beautiful things to say in the *Gita*. And Lao-Tzu had some tremendous things to say in *The Way of Life*. And Confucius had some neat things to say. But all of them suffered a terrible fate, the same fate that another great man suffered, a man by the name of Jesus. No, they weren't all crucified. That isn't the worst thing that happened to Jesus. The worst thing that ever happened to Him was that a religion was formed about Him; the worst possible thing that could ever be done to anybody who comes with a message.

Have you ever heard about the five M's? Do you know what the five M's are? – man, message, movement, machine, monument. And how often has this happened, that a man has come to say, 'I am love and I am truth and I am life and what is true about me is true about you; what I am, you are.' And instead of following that, there has been the putting of these men on a pedestal: 'I'm just human, don't expect too much of me. He's divine, but I'm just human.' And yet every one of these enlightened ones who came into the world said, 'I'm the light of the world; you are the light of the world. Let that which you are be expressed.' And yet what do people do? 'I'm a sinner.' If you think you're a sinner you are a sinner. It's as simple as that. You can never express anything greater than your image.

But it is not a matter of imagining it, of sitting there and saying, 'I am imagining that I am God, light and truth.' That's imagina-tion; you are tricking yourself. You only know, not what you imagine but what you express. Then you begin to have a sensing that the underworld is not the place for you, that your feelings and thoughts, the structures that are a result of your conditioning, are a false identity. It is not the truth of you. It is a conditioned self; it is not you. And you begin to have a sense that that which you are transcends that which you have, and that which you are dwells here in heaven on earth. Jesus said it so beautifully: 'Thy kingdom come. Thy will be done in earth, as it is in heaven.' Heaven isn't some place you go to. It is the state of consciousness that in reality the spirit that you are, the unconditional reality, is already dwelling in. But it needs to dwell consciously in the body and in the mind and in the feeling realm, because it deeply desires to allow these qualities to be expressed through these capacities into the earth. And when heaven and earth are one in that way, then the body and mind and feeling realm come back into balance. You can obtain some sense of balance by moving out of the extreme of the human nature consciousness, but you don't know what real balance is until you move out of the balance place in the human nature state and move into the crossover point, the balance in one's own true nature, in heaven on earth. And when that begins to happen, your particular earth begins to be a reflection of your own heaven.

'But George, I've always been taught all my life . . . I've been programed . . . You can't expect me to . . .' We need balanced persons here and now if the world is to be restored, if the world is to take its rightful place in the cosmos and fulfil the cosmic purposes that it was created to fulfil. But it takes people willing to accept the responsibility of being all that they really are, so that they can get on with doing what they came into the earth to do.

Accept the responsibility. And it's done in the little things, you know. The true artist isn't just the one sitting down at a canvas. The true artist in life is an expert in spiritual expression in the bathroom as well, for instance. In other words, if he should find four pieces of toilet tissue left on the roll, he doesn't get up and go his way so somebody else sitting down has to say, 'Where's the toilet tissue?' Not on your cotton-picking! This man deeply desires the best for whoever comes after him. So he goes and gets a roll, takes the paper off the roll and puts it in the wastebasket, and then actually puts the roll on the dispenser – carries clear through in every aspect of his living. And because he does it in the bathroom, he can be creative when he gets in front of a canvas, or whatever. If you ain't creative in your everyday living you ain't going to be creative when you sit down at a canvas or piano or anything else! This is a prerequisite for any creative living.

This is why I'm excited about the Emissary Society. It has taught me the art of creative living. It has helped me to see, not so much by precept but by example, what it means to sound a clear tone. Up until 1970 I compared my tone with other tones and they were about the same. So I thought, 'That's the only tone to sound.' Do you know that story about little Hunter, the guy in the comic strip who is four-and-a-half years old? He comes in and sees little Julian playing the violin. And Julian looks up and says, 'Tiger, I'm playing variations on a theme by Bach.' And Sally comes in and asks, 'Tiger, what's Julian doing?' And Tiger says, 'Julian is playing violations of a theme by Bach.'

You know, you and I have come to play a variation of a great theme, a balanced note which would bring a chord, a harmony, into the world. But because we have been born into a world where the vast majority of people are living in the underworld and not the overworld, because they haven't known the truth of themselves, we have grown up thinking that we were the result of our heredity and our environment and our reactions, and that the note we were sounding was the only note that could be sounded.

I found a quality of living seven years ago, such a clear note, that I began to see that my note was pretty sour and that I needed to let that sour note go, that I needed to let go of concepts and beliefs and so many of the things that were out of my conditioned past; I needed to let it all go and move to a place where I could discover the unconditional quality of love, because I love to express those spirits through my capacities. And there were those people around me who were drawing that forth from me, at Sunrise Ranch and at other centers of the Emissary Society.

What is an Emissary? A person who has a sense that 'I've come into the world to sound the right tone, to express my totality, to let my light shine in the right way.' But every single person that I meet is in truth an Emissary. We all came into the earth to find a body, mind and heart through which we could express the qualities of the overworld. I see that as the truth of every one of you. And I celebrate whatever it is in your life that has brought you to the place where you are seeing to your highest vision and expressing that which seems appropriate to you.

Something is happening in the world. There are centers, communities of life, communities where spiritual expression, because of spiritual orientation, is the primary concern. But many people say to me, 'George, these communities around the world are impressive, but look at all the problems in the world. Any way you look the world is disintegrating. Is there any hope that the world can be a world of integration instead of a world of disintegration?' Well I would like to share a passage out of a book called *Rhythms of Vision*. This one little story may give you some idea of what it means when I speak of sounding the tone, and that it is the sounding of that tone not by the vast majority of people necessarily but by enough people who are really doing it in their living that is going to make the difference. Let me read you this little story:

> Off the coast of Japan are a number of tiny islands where resident populations of macaques have been under continuous observation for more than twenty years. The scientists provide supplementary food, but the monkeys also feed themselves by digging up sweet potatoes and eating them dirt and all. This uncomfortable practice continued unchanged for many years until one day a young male monkey broke with tradition and carried his potato down to the sea where he washed it before eating it. He taught the trick to his mother, who showed it to her current mate and so the culture spread through the colony until most of them, let us say 99 monkeys, were doing it. Then one Tuesday morning at eleven, the hundredth individual acquired the habit and, within an hour, it appeared on two other islands in two physically unconnected populations of monkeys who until that moment had shown no inclination to wash their food.

And the writer says:

> I believe that ideas in human societies spread in the same kind of way and that when enough of us hold something to be true, then it becomes true for everyone.

It is a matter of being held not by concepts and beliefs but by allowing the conscious and subconscious mind to be held by the spirit of the truth of love that I am and you are in reality. Now there are many, many possibilities of what the next step might be for you. In the seven years that I have been offering the possibility of the next step, I've never found anyone who deeply desired to know what the next step was who didn't find it where they needed to find it. And then taking that next step, they found the next step. And then, when we are expressing those right thoughts, appropriate concerns, in our everyday, practical living, we join with others who are sounding a clear tone. And it is the sounding of that clear tone that will restore the individual to balance in the world today.

A talk given at the Westlake National Bank, Loveland, Colorado, May 1977.

THEODORE BLACK, a Canadian by birth, is a graduate of the University of Manitoba, with degrees in Science and Education. He taught high school for a number of years in Canada before moving to Colorado.

He lives presently at Sunrise Ranch. He is associate editor of a quarterly magazine published there by Eden Valley Press – *The Emissary*, a journal dedicated to the practical art of living.

Mr. Black has done much public speaking in recent years, addressing service clubs, university student groups, and classes in philosophy and psychology. He has also participated in symposia and seminars in various parts of the country, and has given much time to individual counseling, encouraging the development of a higher consciousness and a true effectiveness in the art of living.

REFLECTIONS OF THE SUPERCONSCIOUS

Theodore Black

It's a great pleasure to be here with you this evening in Fort Wayne. On our way east we passed through Indiana, the northern tip of it, and stopped to visit some friends along Lake Michigan. On this return trip we have had opportunity to be in your lovely state for a little longer. We spent a couple of days at Rainbow Farm, a place that we have in central Indiana, near Muncie. I say 'we' because it is an Emissary center; some of you may know Mac and Jane Duff, who live there. They are presently having a week seminar – not a weak seminar but a very strong seminar. And we participated in the first day of that.

So here we are now in Fort Wayne, Indiana, and about (tomorrow) to move out of this state. But I trust we shall all still be present in the state of life, which is very much in evidence here this evening because there are people present in this room who are in the state of life, the state of living, an on-going state, a state of this moment, and the next moment, and the next. It is interesting, that matter of moments. As soon as you say 'this moment' it is past. So we have to keep moving. Want to stop moving? Well lie down and die; it is the only way. As long as we are alive we are moving from moment to moment; from place to place too, for that matter, because even if we are sitting very still we are moving with the planet about the sun at a rate of about 18 miles per second. And in that movement we find ourselves spiraling through space, never actually returning to the same spot again. Even though in the yearly circling round we come back again to the same side of the sun, because the sun has moved we are not at the same point in space. Always there is onward movement.

So it is interesting to observe this, but more than interesting it is needful that we begin to have a sense of who we are and where we are, on this planet spiraling through space, because if we don't have a sense of who we are and where we are, and why we are here where we are, we don't really participate in the livingness possible to us in this moment and each succeeding moment. In a sense that is a mistaken way of viewing it, as succeeding moments, because where is the division? How do you say this is one moment and then this is the next moment? What's in between? No moments? But there are some moments in between; there is a continuity. In fact we never leave the present moment; we remain in the present moment and time, whatever it is, passes us by, or passes through us. Here again it is a matter of how we view what is happening. Many people, I think most of us from time to time, have the feeling that life is passing us by. And sure enough, it is passing us by because of the attitude we are taking. Yet if we come to for a moment we sense that in actuality life isn't passing us by. We are alive; we're here in this moment, which continues to be this moment. Have you ever experienced a time when it wasn't this moment? Have you ever experienced the past? You may say, 'Something happened to me ten minutes ago; I came into this room.' Oh? How do you know? That is an imagination, really, now. We may think that such and such happened in the past, and it may be a useful fiction giving us a sense of continuity in our movement, but in actual fact what is real to us is that we are here now. Undoubtedly something did happen ten or fifteen minutes ago and we found ourselves entering this room by whatever means we came in; we are here. And undoubtedly an hour or so hence we will go out from this room. Yet all that past/present/future business really has no meaning except as we sense a continuity with the presence of life right now in this very minute.

Now, I preface what I have to say this evening with those words because it is important that we sense that we are here now, and that no matter what has happened in the past, no matter what may happen in the future, the important thing for us now is that we are here now, we are alive here now, together, sharing the experience of life in this room, wherever that may be in the universe. We are in fact never anything but here present because only in the present moment do we live. We may have some imagination that we had an experience in the past, we may have some imagination that some experience is coming out of the future, but we only actually know the experience now.

History, whether it is the record of the human race – political histories or biographies – or whether it is our own personal history, our own memory of what took place, always is to some extent fictional because we don't actually remember just the way it happened. Do you, as far as your coming into the room ten or fifteen minutes ago, know exactly at what point your left foot touched the carpet and then your right foot? Could you go back and trace out a diagram of where your feet touched down, of what molecules of air entered your lungs and then were expelled, of what the complete situation was? No. Our memories are very, very partial. Experiments have been conducted – I don't recall by whom; Penfield, I think it was (there, a name out of the past!) – in any case, he found that by stimulating certain areas of a patient's brain he could induce total recall of events. 'On July 26, 1948, I was walking down Telfer Street in the town of Wabash, and I saw a cardinal sitting in a tree and a dog ran down the walk in front of a white house' – this sort of thing would pop up into consciousness, something the man ordinarily couldn't remember. Now, the theory developed consequently that everything is recorded. Well perhaps there is the recording in our subconscious realm of the experience that we have consciously had over the years; something has come in through the conscious mind and been recorded in the subconscious. And this may be stimulated into recall, either medically or as happened to me a moment ago with the name Penfield – which I am almost certain is not the correct name! But however it may happen, this in itself is only a superficial recall, because that person whose brain was stimulated into describing all the personal experiences of that day in the past was only recalling what had been observed consciously. He could not have told you what position in the universe the earth occupied at that time. Much, in other words, was actually happening which was not present to his conscious mind and therefore was not recorded. So, again, recall is fiction because it is only a partial story. The most 'perfect' total recall is still only a partial story. Yet in this present moment we are in actual fact experiencing the totality of living presence in this universe. Present to us in this moment in this particular spot in the universe is the experience of life throughout the universe, coming to focus for each one of us exactly where we are now.

Now the reason that historical or personal recall is incomplete and therefore to that extent fictional is that the conscious mind, which has allowed the flow into the subconscious and allows the flow out through the pen onto the records, is only the smallest portion of the capacity to experience life. What is recalled is only a small part of what the conscious mind experienced, and the conscious mind in each moment knows only a small part of the total experience of the individual. We in this moment are having a much, much vaster experience than our conscious minds might lead us to believe.

One of the titles I've been using for various public talks during this little tour is 'Beyond the Surface Consciousness.' What I have just said during the last ten minutes here was not said in any one of those talks, and where it came from I have consciously no idea. I hadn't intended to start off talking about the present moment and consciousness and recall, and all the rest of it. So it evidently is something of the experience of this present moment that was in no sense prepared for by my conscious mind. However, be that as it may, we together here in this room are having an experience. To what extent that experience is conscious, to what extent that experience is a unified and really creative one, will depend upon the attitude we take toward the experience of this present moment. It will also depend to some extent on the capacity we have developed for present living experience.

There is a level of our being at which we are in total touch with everything that is happening in the universe, but as far as our conscious experience in this present moment is concerned we touch only the thinnest layer of that. In an example I've been using in some of my talks I have compared it to the experience of being the surface of this glass of water. It is so thin a layer that in effect it isn't really there. It is only a division plane between the water and the air. If I drink the water down, the surface disappears; there would be no surface but for the water. So the surface implies the presence of some water. The surface consciousness, which is the aspect of consciousness of which we are aware in the immediate experience of our conscious mind, is only there because of the presence of much, much more. There is a subconscious. And of course, if there is a surface there must be something above it. In the example of the glass of water there is air above the surface. So here we have a very simple analogy with respect to realms of consciousness. You have three distinct and yet not separate levels of experience: there is the air, there is the surface of the water, there is the water itself underneath. Similarly, in respect to human capacity, we have the surface consciousness of our immediate experience, we have the subconscious, and we have most definitely something above the conscious mind, the superconscious we might call it, well symbolized by the air.

Considering the glass of water, you can see rather vividly that there is a lot more air than there is water in the glass and surface of that water. And this again is a very apt analogy of the individual conscious and subconscious mind and the presence of the superconscious, which we might also speak of as air, the air of the spirit. The purpose of the conscious mind is to present a clear surface to the presence of the air of the spirit. And if there is a calmness in the conscious state, if the waters are not all wavy and in turmoil, then there may be, as is the case with water, a reflection of something present in the air round about. If there is a calmness in the conscious mind then it may be possible to experience a reflection of what is far beyond the conscious mind. And because of that there may be – the analogy begins to break down a little here – there may be the absorption into the subconscious realm of an imprint of what has happened at the conscious level, an imprint of that reflection of what is in the air of the spirit above the conscious level. The subconscious may participate in that and there may be memory in the subconscious realm which may prove useful at a later period of time. The usefulness is always in regard to there being the balance of these three levels: the subconscious, the conscious, and the superconscious.

Human beings have generally been very much aware of the con-

scious mind. 'With my conscious mind I'm going to do this and
I'm going to do that and I'm going to do the other thing. I'm going
to think great thoughts and achieve great things. And of course I
understand that this is based in what I can use out of my subconscious. Therefore I'm going to have to put a lot into that subconscious through various methods of education, so that I will have
a great store of knowledge to use in achieving what my conscious
mind wants to achieve.' But scarcely any real consideration is
given to the fact that there is vastly more present in the immediate
experience than either the conscious or subconscious mind of the
individual. There is the vastness of the atmosphere, in this analogy. There is the vastness of the superconscious, the vastness of
the connecting atmosphere of spirit, which, for one thing, allows
a connection between a number of glasses of water. You may, for
example, set up sound waves in one glass of water which may be
communicated to another glass of water, but only if there is air
present between them. Only if there is the air of the spirit present,
only if we are sufficiently in touch with the connecting atmosphere
of the spirit, can we actually communicate with one another. I
might talk myself blue in the face – which I don't intend to do, but
I might – and actually achieve no communication to you if there
were not present the air of the spirit as a connection between us
and if we were not, each of us, sufficiently open to that to provide
a line of connection through that air of the spirit.

Now, the air of the spirit is always present; there is no question
about that. The superconscious is always present. However human
beings have tended to limit themselves from this. There are various ways we close ourselves off from the experience of life. 'I don't
want it! I want to have my own little world.' People shut themselves off from one another that way, don't they? They decide that
they don't want to have the experience which seems to be coming
up. You see somebody coming down the street and you duck
around a corner so you won't have a connection with that person.
You still have, by the way. Ducking around the corner doesn't
eliminate a connection. If you've ducked around the corner because
you are afraid of meeting that person, or you don't want to for
some reason or other, you already have a heart-to-heart vibrational

contact, which is probably a vibration of fear, or a vibration of dislike, or whatever other unhealthy emotion may be present in your heart. And the very fact of ducking around the corner to avoid the person means that you have built that connection, on a wrong basis, even stronger. Far from actually avoiding the unpleasantness, you have made the inevitable meeting much worse when it does come about.

There is the story about a fellow who was reluctant to go to school one day. He was lying in bed, unwilling to get up, unwilling to wash his face and have his breakfast eggs and get off to school. And he was saying to his mother, 'I can give you two reasons why it is just too much for me to go to school today. One is, the kids all hate me; and the other reason is, the teachers all hate me.' And the mother said to him, 'Well son, I'll give you two reasons why you ought to go to school this morning. One is, you're forty-seven years old; and the other is, you are the principal.' That one has a degree of fundamental truth that hurts. I have never been the principal of a school but I used to teach, and I know the feeling. In those dim and distant days in the past, which I vaguely remember according to the historical fiction means I was speaking of, I can recall having some pretty heartsick feelings about going to school and being a teacher. And I can also recall the principal looking as if he had about ten times as many heartsick feelings. The kids of course didn't like it much either. They were like the little boy who said he didn't mind school, the actual experience of it, it was just the principal of the thing. So, in any case, because we have these nasty feelings about what is going on in the world about us we tend to block off the atmosphere of connection. Now, the atmosphere of connection between us may have been somewhat polluted, as human beings are fond of polluting their atmosphere. They pollute it in these days, in the physical sense, with all sorts of exhaust of one kind or another. And they pollute the vibrational atmosphere with exhaust too; hot air, you call it, when people spill off what happens to be in their subconscious. The atmosphere in many different ways has been polluted in the vicinity of human beings. However the atmosphere is at least present, even though polluted, round about human beings, and is present to be the means for the connection that we may have with one another. That is not its only reason for being present but it is the only way we have the potential of a right connection with one another.

On a TV talk show this morning the interviewer asked me whether at Sunrise Ranch we were concerned about other people and the things in our environment. I said, 'Yes, very much, there is an attitude of caring, not only for the people but the animals, the plants, the rocks in our environment.' There is in other words an outreach of concern. However there is something else to it too. I wasn't able to go into any great detail on this very brief television show, but when we speak of having a concern for one another, well many people have a concern for one another. And there are those altruistic souls who have a concern for the whole human race: 'I love the human race.' Generally they don't particularly like sister Becky, but they love the whole human race; they love it in the abstract. Like the man who was laying the cement sidewalk, and little Johnny ran through it. He picked up little Johnny and walloped him. The mother came out and said, 'I thought you loved children.' 'Oh, yes,' he said, 'I love them in the abstract, but I do not love them in the concrete.'

The fact is that human beings find it difficult to actually communicate their great love for one another because, here again, it stops short; there is a wall of limitation put up. The word *ecology* is bandied about a great deal these days. Human beings say, 'I'm very concerned about the ecology. I want the plants and animals to be living together in a correct and symbolic relationship with me.' Some very wise individuals actually see themselves as part of the ecology. Most don't; they see the ecology as just being all the stuff out there. But in either case the attitude generally is: 'We want the ecology to be just right because human beings are sadly harmed by the way in which other human beings have harmed the environment. "They" did it to us; now we are going to be very generous and help people to clean up the environment. Maybe we will even take a little responsibility for some of the pollution we put into it. But we are going to clean it up so it will be a nice place for *us*, or so that it will be a nice place for all mankind.' But you know, even if our altruism extends to include the whole human race, it is still extremely self-centered because it is just the human race, just that. We are not aware, apparently, of the fact that we exist within an atmosphere which goes on forever, that we are present within a life system which includes at least all of the known universe, and more beyond that.

Now, we cannot function with a total conscious comprehension of the whole universe. If even all that is going on on the surface of this earth were to be, in this instant, consciously opened to our minds we would go insane immediately with the weight of it all. Let us be thankful that our conscious minds cannot take it all in. So I'm not talking about trying to consciously comprehend all that is going on in the universe but rather about an attitude that recognizes we are part of something else than just our own little human affairs. In the January issue of this magazine, *The Emissary*, we had a consideration of solar. You know, there is a lot of interest these days in solar energy and in how this can be used for human beings. That is about the extent of what the consideration of solar energy tends to be, how it can be used to benefit human beings. Well, I would submit that the sun is not present just to benefit human beings. Again, it is a matter of attitude. I'm not saying there is anything wrong with having solar energy units. What is wrong is how we approach this, on the basis of grabbing something for ourselves. 'Look at all this energy going to waste. The sun is spreading energy throughout the universe; the earth catches only a tiny part of it. Well let's at least try to trap some of this and use it before it gets away from us.' Get! Get! Get! In the human consciousness everything is getting away on us. 'Life is passing me by! I've got to grab it while the grabbing's good!' The greed consciousness. And along with it the fear consciousness. This is what has produced the polluted state in the world of human beings.

I would submit that the only way we can approach a really creative experience, a living experience, is to begin to change our attitude, to begin to see that we are not the whole cheese. We are very, very small peanuts in this universe. And yet we are part of it; we are a living part of it. It is important that we learn to cooperate with what is going on so that we can be a useful part of it. If we are not a useful part of it, good-bye! I mean, what's the sense of keeping people around who are constantly on strike? No sane factory owner would keep on the payroll a staff, or a working force, which for the last fifty years has been on strike. An altruistic factory owner might say, 'Well I'll let them go on strike for a little while; maybe I'll even meet their demands.' But to go on strike for fifty years and expect to still be paid? Human beings have been on strike for a lot longer than fifty years; for a good many generations in fact, on strike against life. And they expect life to continue paying with the living experience. It doesn't work that way! Human beings die individually, and the human race might die collectively because of this attitude. The only answer to it is to give up the striking attitude, this striking pose, and reenter the business of living; come back into the factory, you might say, and pick up our tools and get to work, cooperating with the actual design and purpose of living here and now.

Well I started to speak about the magazine. For the January issue I wrote an article entitled 'Beyond the Surface Consciousness.' Along with it we printed a photograph of a girl among trees bathed in sunlight. The caption under it was a quote from the article: 'We are part of a wholeness – that is the reality.' What I loved about this photograph when I first saw it, and the reason I used it in this context, was that while you are aware of this girl and her face up to the sun, you are also aware that it is very difficult to see where her form leaves off and the surround takes over in the picture, where the tree ends and the face begins. There is a very distinguishable face there; there is a focus of human living. But there is also a focus of tree living and a focus of atmospheric conditions there. It all blends together in this picture, coming to focus in the human being but without a sense of division. And it is this consciousness we need to develop. We are individuals, yes. It is not a case of being a drop in the ocean of life. There has been some concept about that in certain religious disciplines, particularly the eastern religions, that the great, the ultimate goal of human beings is to be a drop in the ocean. What use is that? I mean, the ocean is useful, but certainly the purpose of human beings is not to lose themselves in the ocean of life. Why would we have been created individuals? We are created individuals because there is something needful for expression through this individuality. However, it isn't a separate individuality; it is the individuality of connection with, properly cooperation with, the totality. There is the universe; it is one thing. Within that universe there are entities which are part of the total entity. We exist in the solar entity; we are living in the sun. In actual fact we are. We are moving in the sun's gravitational field, and in its electromagnetic field. 'But the sun is 93 million miles away.' Who said so? Is what you can see of the sun all there is to it? If that were so then there would be no connection between us and the sun. But there is a connection; there is light. 'Well,' you say, 'that comes to us from the sun.' That may be a way of looking at it, but I would say that that is the way of looking at it that has been traditional in the separatist consciousness of human beings. In actual fact we are in the sun. One of the aspects of being in the sun, at the particular position in it where the earth is found, is that we are bathed with the radiance of the sun. We are bathed with the gravitational influence of the sun. We are bathed with the electromagnetic influence, a beautiful presence of life which we see in its focal point as what we call the visible sun, far away. But the totality of this solar entity is not at all far away; we are in it in fact. The earth is in it and we are part of the total living expression of this earth within the total living expression of the solar entity, the solar system consisting of other parts, the other planets, swimming in this solar sea and connected with the vibrational atmosphere of other stars and star systems within the galaxy, which is connected with the vibrational atmosphere of other galaxies. And so on out; the whole universe is one thing. And we are in that. If we continue to see ourselves separate then eventually we prove our separateness, because human beings, on that basis, die. In actual fact nothing is lost to life; it comes up as daffodils. There is a regeneration and a re-use of the substance. But the human entity, the human conscious entity, is gone because it stayed on strike too long. We need to come back to work; we need to be willing to be present with life, actually participating in the total function of the living entity. There is much analysis about what is present in the universe. I've talked here a bit about the sun and the stars, and so forth. Many learned men have looked at these things.

I was just reading this afternoon, in an issue of the magazine *Natural History*, that consequent upon recent investigations of what is present on the sun, scientists are beginning to sense that they really don't know what it is all about; they really don't know how the sun functions. It is an amazing admission. But, really, we don't need to go searching for more knowledge; we need first of all to begin to find ourselves.

Sensing the fact of life, sensing the eternal and infinite presence of life, in silence, with a calm, tranquil face of the water, the surface of consciousness, presented to the totality of life expression in the universe, we may begin to know what it is all about, what it is all about insofar as we are concerned, why we are here, what it is of life we have to express in this moment. It does not come from stirring up the waters like mad, getting the surface all ruffled up with effort to understand it all. It comes from realizing that we are part of it all and that such understanding as the conscious mind needs will be reflected in the conscious mind when that calm surface is presented to the influence of life, when the atmosphere of the spirit of life is allowed to touch our surface at all points easily, smoothly. And when we cease attempting to pollute that atmosphere with our rotten froth of surface pollution then we may experience life as it is here and now. On that basis we not only know something about ourselves and our place in the universe but we have a keen sensing of one another. We have a keener awareness of what is needed in our relationships with one another, how to rightly care for one another, and care for all the circumstances in our environment. We can't know that by all the analysis of the human mind; we can know it when the mind is allowed to be what it should be – a calm and clear instrument for the reflection of what is present in the spirit of life.

A talk given in Fort Wayne, Indiana, April 12, 1977.

RECEIVING LIFE

Theodore Black

There is a passage in the Book of Mark which tells of Jesus' attitude toward children:

'And they brought young children to him, that he should touch them: and his disciples rebuked those that brought them.

'But when Jesus saw it, he was much displeased, and said unto them, Suffer the little children to come unto me, and forbid them not: for of such is the kingdom of God.

'Verily I say unto you, Whosoever shall not receive the kingdom of God as a little child, he shall not enter therein.

'And he took them up in his arms, put his hands upon them and blessed them.'

'Whosoever shall not receive the kingdom of God as a little child, he shall not enter therein.' I think it tends to be imagined by most people that the kingdom of God is some sort of blessed state that we will go to one day. Generally in the Christian considerations that day is after we die; then we will graduate to heaven. I'm not just sure why we would think that we could graduate to heaven, not having passed the examination. Life examines us continually to see of what stuff we are, and people continually fail the examination, don't they? – don't we? – fail to live up to the command of life to be as life, creative, giving, outpouring. We're in the season of the year now when the wind blows and the waters flow and the leaves begin to burst forth on the trees, and you see this happening, a revelation of what is happening internally in the tree – the sap is rising. Some are tapping the sap from the maple trees to make that delicious maple syrup. We know the sap is rising and the buds are just getting ready to burst. And we see this process happening in that way and in many other ways, through plants and animals, through ourselves too, the continual physical development. As a child grows the expansion takes place, the bursting out. And physically this is very obviously the movement of life, an expansion and a bursting forth of the energy and flow of life. In all my years of watching leaves pop forth on the trees, I've never yet seen a tree decide to retract its leaves: out they came and the tree decided that it wasn't worth giving forth anything of living expression into this awful world, and so it pulled its leaves back in again. Have you ever seen that happen? You've seen it happen with human beings though, haven't you? 'Once bit, twice shy,' they say. 'Once upon a time I said a kind word to somebody and the reply was so nasty that . . . never again, that's it, I'm done with it! I'm done with that person; I'm fed up. I'm not going to express anything kindly or supportive to that person again. Just once too many. I've had it.' And we close off, we decide not to give forth the expression of life.

Or else we go around slurping up all we can possibly get from the environment. We read books that describe how to get more out of your twenty-four hours, how to get more out of living, how to clear the 'erroneous zones' from your character so that you will have yourself a more delightful experience. They are all very logical and very reasonable bits of advice. And it works after a fashion. You agree with the principles of life to the extent that is necessary in order that you may receive an immediate return and have a pleasant experience; or you agree with some sort of principles, perhaps religious principles, which will enable you to insure for yourself a place in the hereafter; or you agree with the scientific principles in such a way that it will insure utopia some day in the future – two cars in the garage and a pension scheme. People will agree with certain basic principles of practical living in order to get what they want out of it. And it depends, I suppose, on the extent of one's vision, how far one will go with this. Some people can see no further than their own immediate main chance, and anything that doesn't affect that just isn't seen. The fact, for example, that the energy resources may be running out – 'What does that matter so long as there is enough oil in the house to keep *me* warm? I've got the two cars in the garage; I've got enough oil for this winter and next winter anyway. Maybe for my lifetime there is enough for me.' Most people think ahead that far – 'I'll sign up on an excellent insurance policy retirement scheme so that *I* will have enough to take care of *me* in my old age.'

Then there are those who think a little further; perhaps they have children, and they consider that maybe something needs to be done for the next generation of human beings. 'We'll be very altruistic, and we'll work hard to make it a better world for the next generation.' I recall that was the slogan during the Second World War; it was a war to make it a better world to live in. Oh, yeah! War will make the world a better world to live in, won't it? Aside from whatever may have been the necessities at that time – it's back in history now – it didn't make a better world. Nothing of that nature, nothing of human being's graspingness or human beings' altruism will make it a better world to live in. There is the good and the bad end of the stick. Some people rob banks in order to make it a better world for them to live in; some people give to charity in order to make it a better world for them to live in – they will rest easier, their conscience salved. But it is all part of the same thing, part of the rotten human state that is not a better world at all. It is a world full of stresses and strains and troubles, and hardly an expression of the kingdom of heaven. But of course the assumption is that the kingdom of heaven isn't present; it would be possible maybe to experience it after one died or in some scientific utopia in the future, but it isn't present now. As I say, it is hard to assess the reasoning that assumes people deserve some sort of heavenly experience in the future on the basis of what they are doing now. We will don our white robes and go floating off into paradise! How long would it stay paradise if we got there? I mean, frankly and honestly, every one of us can look at that in terms of our own expression at the present time. Is it such that paradise would be enhanced by our presence? I rather doubt it.

However, the kingdom of heaven is in fact, as our Master emphasized over and over again, at hand, right here. Now where is 'at hand'? I can reach out and touch this glass of water. Okay, there is the kingdom of heaven, at hand. Collectively we can reach out and touch quite a bit. How far can we touch vibrationally?

The kingdom of heaven is there. The kingdom of heaven is at hand, as close as this glass of water – getting closer, getting closer. My hand can come pretty close to me, and the kingdom of heaven is at hand. Where does it stop? We have tended to think of 'at hand' as meaning just around the corner. Around what corner? Is your hand reaching around the corner somewhere? If there is any meaning in that statement at all it is that the kingdom of heaven is present; the control factors for the experience of heaven on earth – in other words the experience of life on earth, the experience of creativity on earth – are present with us, inherent in the character of our reality. It is that close. It is so close that nothing is closer. Life is close, isn't it? We are alive. True, there is no place in the living universe where life is not. But as far as our experience is concerned the kingdom of heaven, the control factors for the expression of life, are present right here. And if we act as if that were not true then we produce the state of the world that human beings know presently, the poisonous, polluted state of what could be termed the insane asylum of the universe, here on the face of this earth, the one place in the living universe where there is some obstruction to the flow of life. That results from the distorted expression of human beings believing that the kingdom of heaven is not here present.

Now, a child, as Jesus was pointing out here, receives the kingdom of God. Note that word *receives*. 'Whosoever shall not receive the kingdom of God as a little child, he shall not enter therein.' Receiving it to oneself. Human beings, particularly in the Christian fold, have prayed for many a century, 'Thy kingdom come,' while constantly and consistently resisting the coming of the kingdom, until finally those who insist upon resisting the coming of the kingdom are eliminated and the kingdom comes. Realize that every time a human being kicks the bucket the kingdom comes, just as the ocean flows in after a shipwreck, because the kingdom of heaven, the reality of the control factors, the design factors, the beauty of life, is present in the universe. The only thing preventing it in the experience of human beings is the attitude of human beings. We can, with great effort, prevent the experience of the kingdom of heaven for ourselves. It is an enormous accomplishment, but it doesn't enable one to pass the examination of life. All this studying, all the effort to manipulate the environment in order to shield ourselves from the pressure of life! People talk about that, don't they? The pressure of life! One has to really struggle to withstand the pressures of life, pressing to come into our experience, pressing to be released therefore out through us into our immediate experience. The pressure in one sense is an internal pressure. In another sense it could be seen as an external pressure; it is external to human beings' present experience because of a wall that has been put up, the hardness of the heart that prevents the inflow of the spirit of life. It is internal in the sense that this pressure of life, of the spirit of life, is an invisible, immaterial pressure – nonetheless real, actually far stronger and more powerful than anything in the material world. But human beings have the power of choice to decide whether or not to allow this pressure of life to be released into their immediate experience. This is the purpose of our existence here. We are here to allow life to express creatively in this specific human way. The trees, as I say, give forth their leaves; they've never thought of doing otherwise. They do not have the human consciousness which would allow the choice not to release life; so they do it, they release the expression of life constantly. The animals do the same. The rocks do the same. Only human beings, for a specific purpose, have the ability to choose whether or not to move with it, because without that ᴏbility we would not be able to participate in the creative movement of life in a knowing, conscious way. We are privileged, in other words, to share in the unique, fresh-in-every-instance, new creativeness of life. That is our privilege. But it is a privilege that we, and generations before us, have consistently thrown away, the privilege of creating heaven in the environment, allowing the flow of heaven in the spirit of life to come in invisibly to be translated in us and released visibly so that it is in fact at hand in the material world. The kingdom of heaven is at hand, vibrationally, with us. It may be at hand in the material sense when we decide to release it.

It is said that the kingdom of God is within you. And human beings search for the kingdom of God. Many wouldn't put it that way; there are many people who say, 'That God thing, I don't know anything about that. I'm an agnostic, or an atheist. I don't believe in that nonsense.' But they go hunting in one way or another for some sort of fulfilment, purpose, meaning, to their lives. It is the same thing; they are hunting for the kingdom of God. They are hunting for, in the external world, fulfilment. But the fulfilment is present in the external world of our environment when we put it there, and not before.

Now, we can to some extent participate in the fulfilment, in the presence of the kingdom of God in the external world, that some-one else has put there. This is of course the privilege and respon-sibility we have in caring for children, because children have not yet the developed ability for spiritual expression, the ability to actually release the kingdom into their experience in this way. And so it is provided for them, or ought to be, so that they have a set-ting in which to grow and learn to consciously release and express the kingdom. They do it unconsciously, even as the trees and the flowers do, but they need to grow into the experience of being full human beings, with the full privileges and responsibilities of that state. But what has been provided for them? What indeed! The child receives, you see. The child receives the kingdom of God constantly; at the subconscious level there is no problem. As the consciousness develops the problems arise because the child, re-ceiving what is provided for it in the present state of human affairs, receives a lot of rottenness into the subconscious. It's poured in; we open the top and pour it in. That is the main experience of educa-tion in today's world, isn't it? Open up the lid and pour it in, and see if the child can regurgitate it onto the test paper. If the child is wise, as most children are in the beginning, he vomits it up and is rid of it. But as time goes on, he sees the value of retaining some of this, so he crams and crams. A lot of it gets lost; a lot of it gets stuffed down into the subconscious. The point is that this rotten-ness which is received along the way produces a state of conscious-ness in which the child, growing up, willingly agrees to resist life. It is an uncomfortable business. And there comes a point some-where along the way between the age of puberty and the age of discretion – whatever that is – in the teens, where there is tremendous rebellion because something is fighting there for release, something of the spirit of life is fighting for release and is being resisted very consciously by the human beings round about – 'We've got to discipline that child! We've got to hold him in line! We've got to show him which is the right way to go!' And also, for the child's own good, 'You've got to learn to fight for yourself in this world, this dog-eat-dog world. You'd better learn the canine tricks. It is a miserable existence you have been born into, and you are just going to have to make the best of it and fight your way, and try to survive.' All this is drummed in. 'And the way to do it, of course, is to get an education, get an education. You can't survive without an education.'

And what is this education? It is all this rotten stuff being poured in – along with some true facts, yes. I'm not saying that all the knowledge that is gained through a university education has no value. But it has no value to a person who does not know who he is. And where is the training in any of our universities or colleges or high schools in the art of living, in the art of knowing who you are, so that you know what to do with all the stuff? Actually it is a very dangerous situation for a person to have an immense amount of knowledge and not know who he is, because he will inevitably use this knowledge destructively; he will inevitably use it to build up the bastions, fortify the castle, and fill the moat against life. And incarcerated in this self-wrought prison, he will eventually die and allow life to flood in and take over. But how ridiculous that we should be born and learn to walk and learn to talk and learn to delightedly release something of the kingdom of heaven in the early years, only to have it thrust upon us more and more and more that we need to resist life, that we need to fight it, to the point of eventually killing ourselves, eventually committing suicide! In fact everyone commits suicide – that's what death is – because of the resistance to the flow of life. Surely we are here for something other than that? This is the fact to which Jesus was pointing in these words, that everyone needs to return to the attitude of the little child who receives, who receives the kingdom of heaven. He receives a good deal else too in the world as it presently is, but there is the openness to receive the kingdom of God and to let that be present in his or her experience. The child at an unconscious level does it, but scarcely anyone grows consistently into the release of that kingdom of God in conscious experience.

Now we have the opportunity, seeing these things, to begin to reverse the direction in our own experience, to stop fighting life. Here is the overwhelming flow of the river of life, and here is puny little man struggling to fight his way upstream. Why not reverse directions and flow with it? 'Oh, it is hard! It's difficult! Oh, you know, if you took that attitude, if you didn't fight your way in life, you'd be killed in an instant.' Would you? Would you? A person who says that hasn't tried it. Remember the story of David and Goliath? David went out to fight this great giant, about ten feet tall, with armor, plated armor all over him, and a great spear and shield. At first David tried to put on the armor Saul gave him in order to fight the giant, and he found that when he put the stuff on he couldn't move with it. So he took the armor off and said, 'I can't wear that.' With his five smooth stones from the brook he went out to meet the giant – not in his own power, not 'Here am I, David, fighting you, Goliath.' That was Goliath's attitude: 'Here am I, Goliath, the mightiest man in the army of the Philistines. No one can face up to me.' But David said, 'Who is this uncircumcised Philistine, that he should defy the armies of the living God?' It wasn't, 'I, David, am going to fight this Philistine,' but rather, 'How dare he defy the armies of the living God, the power of the whole universe?' I mean, it was insane! I'm sure that if David could have had the chance to get near enough to talk to Goliath he would have said, 'Come off it, fellow, you haven't got a chance!' And I've often thought that when the stone actually hit Goliath and down he went, it wasn't so much the stone that killed him but the weight of the armor when he fell. This is what kills human beings, all the defensive armor. But David, lightly moving, free of that encumbrance, was able to do what needed to be done at the moment. I'm sure he didn't long to kill giants. But life had to move, and it had to move principally through David. There was a destiny in him to provide a point for the release of life, a point of gathering for other people to begin to flow with this, together. And in order for this to be accomplished certain resistances had to be eliminated.

Sometimes it is thought that if we move with the principles of life everything will immediately come into apple-pie order all round, while we sit watching it all happen, because of course we're so good. We're moving with life, and as a reward we will receive heaven. That's the same old tripe that has been offered to human beings by other human beings who have failed in it all along. Every generation of human beings has tried out this method and found it to fail, and so they teach it to their children. 'One of these days it is going to work' – but it never will! The only thing that will work is revealed as there begin to be human beings willing to receive the kingdom as a little child and to become aware therefore of their own reality, aware of the agreement that may be shared, that has to be shared because it is the nature of life, between real people. As I say, there will be resistances to this because human beings are in the habit of resisting life. It is an obnoxious habit. I recall – maybe some of you remember – a few years back in the 'Li'l Abner' strip, there was a series that went on for several months. Li'l Abner was looking for a cousin of his who had an obnoxious habit. And he was curious to find out what this obnoxious habit was. Eventually – this was carried on in the comic strip for many weeks – Li'l Abner caught up with the fellow with the obnoxious habit, and he was wearing a very loud, red riding habit. And Li'l Abner said, 'Yes, that is an obnoxious habit.' But it is something human beings put on, isn't it? We school ourselves in putting on the armor, the obnoxious habit of human nature expression, thinking that it is protecting us. It is not protecting us from any of the dangers; it is simply shielding out the expression of life through us which would handle the situations.

Now, the situations are handled through human beings who are willing to shed these obnoxious habits and in fact, in every instant, to accept the habit of life, the total attitude and character of life. Then, agreeing together in this attitude, we may bring the power of life to focus on the situation. This is exactly what David did; he had at that moment some agreement, even from Saul. After all,

Saul wanted Goliath eliminated, so if there was any chance that even this young lad could do it, well more power to him! And the army of Israel was right with him, cheering him on. So there was some agreement. Now you might say, 'Well, the army of the Philistines was cheering on Goliath.' Yes, but not in the reality of true agreement. Human beings trying to agree, trying to work together to accomplish their nefarious purposes, are constantly divided; they cannot really know what true agreement is. Only as there is a beginning awareness of one's real identity can agreement really happen, agreement in the spirit of life. As that happened with David in that instance, immense power came to focus, and he didn't need the five stones – the first one did the job. It struck Goliath in the forehead, the seat of intelligence, the point of vulnerability in human beings. For it is the conscious mind in human beings that has been the tool for building the resistances to life. That being eliminated, life flows in. Now, there are two ways in which it can be eliminated. In Goliath's case it occurred with the elimination of the physical form of Goliath, and then life flowed, and David and those with him moved on. But there is another choice, always. We can allow the vulnerable point to be touched by life and all the rotten habits removed, and then there is no more vulnerability because this mind, instead of being open to all the disasters, is open to the power of life, the total power of life, the power of the armies of the living God. And as this is released out, what could possibly hurt? Turn on the faucet and the water flows out; you can't shove mud back up into a faucet where the water is flowing. So indeed, as the life expression is pouring out through us, nothing can get back in; there is nothing of the human state that can possibly resist this flow of life successfully.

Well, we can agree on that. Sitting here today we can nod our heads in agreement and say, 'Yes, that is the way it is.' But how is it come Monday morning? What is it in our experience? Do we find that the bitter battle comes upon us again, and without thinking about it we put up our dukes and start fighting our way through instead of bringing something to point of the spirit of life which handles the situation? We blow it all and start having to fend for ourselves in human strength because everything is washing over us again, all the difficulties – is that the experience on occasion? It is, of course, on occasion the experience, not because it needs to be but because we deliberately decided to cease receiving the kingdom of God. And in the instant that you cease receiving the kingdom of God all your good deeds in the past are as nothing. Because it isn't a matter of reward for good deeds; it is simply a matter of doing the job right. You may drive from San Francisco to New York keeping in the proper lane of traffic; no problems. You have driven all that way, you are a good boy or girl, you've accomplished that drive, and coming into New York you make a left turn onto a one-way street going the other direction and you get clobbered. All the good driving across the country made not the slightest whit of difference. You got clobbered because in the instant you were not with it. Right? Well it is exactly the same thing with all the experience of life. There is no such thing as building up a store of seniority, as it were.

Consistency in the easy way, that's all it is. I mean, why would one, swimming easily with the flow of life, deliberately turn about and try to fight it? 'Oh, but look at this horrible thing coming up, this waterfall. If I flow with life I am going to go over that waterfall; I'm going to be damaged. I'll have to fight it.' Imagination, fancy, fantasies. No, keep flowing; keep moving with life. And through you the power of life will come to point. It is a tremendous pressure, sometimes; there is a job to be done. You know, if you are lifting weights the muscles tense up, don't they? You can't flabbily lift the weight. Life isn't a flabby experience. There are times when everything comes to point through you and the job is done. And if in that instant you duck out – 'Oh, this pressure. I can't stand this pressure' – then you fail. The fact is you're the pressure. What you're saying is 'I can't stand me; let me get out of the way of me!' You are beside yourself. That is literally what insanity is, isn't it? – being beside oneself because one can't stand the pressure of who one is. Ridiculous! Just keep going in the power of the armies of the living God – which is in fact you, your character and your expression. And as we share in the agreement to allow the job of life to be done, that's it; it is done. It is done consistently, moment by moment. And we may look out in the world and see many terrible things going on. But all these terrible things are really not all that terrible after all, because all things are in truth working together to the fulfilment of the design of life, clearing the stage for the next act. And those who are willing to participate in the clearing of the stage will be present for the next act, knowing who they are, ready to do what needs to be done, playing it by the script instead of fighting it and getting knocked off into the aisles and finished.

A talk given at Lake Rest Hotel, Livingston Manor, New York, April 3, 1977.

JAMES WELLEMEYER is a native of Indiana. He served in the Navy during World War II, after which he attended Palmer College of Chiropractic.

For the past fifteen years Mr. Wellemeyer has been director of Sunrise Ranch, the international headquarters of the Society of Emissaries, near Loveland, Colorado. Sunrise Ranch is a community of about 160 men, women and children which provides a living orientation for a rapidly expanding association throughout the world.

Mr. Wellemeyer is an instructor and counselor in the Emissary Training School held at the Ranch, besides being responsible for a number of groups of Emissaries developing in cities in the Rocky Mountain region.

LIGHT AT THE END OF THE TUNNEL

James Wellemeyer

We'll continue with our considerations of the science of being and begin to note how these various laws and principles relate to us. Also this evening perhaps we can begin to see the tremendous responsibility which we have in letting these things be experienced in and through ourselves and recognizing that perhaps there is far more to this thing which we call life than we have actually thought before.

This evening as we gather together we are probably all aware that the President of our country is giving a talk and that he is going to outline certain things in relationship to Vietnam. I wonder if anyone here thinks that what he has to say is going to solve the problem. I suppose we could say that we hope so, wouldn't we? We would like to feel that the words the President utters tonight are going to solve the problem; yet it is highly questionable that they will. I note that Senate Democratic Leader Mike Mansfield has said, 'Great hopes and expectations are riding on this speech. I'm just living on a hope and a prayer that he will offer the American people some light at the end of the tunnel.' At least there is the recognition that there is a tunnel. But this doesn't relate just to the Vietnam situation; it relates to the overall experience of mankind. He is coming to recognize that there is a tunnel. There is the well-worn rut in which man finds himself, and with all his scientific endeavors he has not been able to remove himself from this rut. We've considered the fact that man is very rapidly coming to a crisis point, and we have seen this on a graph showing how we have these different so-called explosions, the population explosion for example. We have noted on our graph that such a situation tends to develop at first very slowly, but now we find that it is going more or less vertically, in what we call an exponential curve. We find that there is really no place to go. We could say we are coming to a stone wall and unless something is done mankind will find that he is going to run right into that wall.

Mansfield recognises that we are in a tunnel and that for the most part, as far as he can see and as far as man can see, there is no knowing in which direction to go. And so what does he have? Hope and a prayer. We often hear said, 'Well prayer is the answer. It solves everything.' Looked at in the true sense this might be the case, but looking at it from the standpoint of the prayers of men and women in the world we must say that it would be questionable because the prayer is usually a begging for something – 'Solve this, solve that!' – instead of being a recognition that man himself is the answer to that prayer, that there is something which can find expression through him which gives the light which Mansfield hopes that Nixon is going to provide this evening. And so in one sense, if we come to see the truth of the matter, we recognize that this light could come not only through President Nixon but through you and through me. In fact this is the only hope which mankind has today.

In our past classes we have been noting that man tends to relate to the things in his environment. He responds to these things, so that they become the most important value to him and if these things aren't present – his car, home, whatever – why then he's badly done by; he can't really get along with other people; he's badly hurt. We could go right down the line listing all these things.

Another article in the paper tonight – about the six skyjackers who returned to the U.S. They had expected to find, I presume, a utopia in Cuba, but they forgot one thing: that they were taking themselves with them. Isn't that right? This one gentleman, a sociologist, one who we would assume could get along with people, found that suddenly he lost his job and shortly thereafter his wife began divorce proceedings and took custody of their daughter. So how did he try to solve the problem? Go to Cuba! And there he was, going to find the light at the end of the tunnel. Then he wrote home to his father that he hated it and they weren't making proper use of his talents. He said the climate was bad, the food wasn't good, and he was practically in jail. Isn't that wonderful! When we see it brought out in this light it seems rather humorous to us, but isn't this what we hear every day? 'The weather's bad. We've never had weather like this; we're setting all kinds of records.' And there is complaint about it. And maybe the food we're getting nowadays isn't good enough. 'Why, they are putting cyclamates in our food,' etc., etc., 'so let's ban it.' And 'Let's ban the bomb.' I'm not saying that they should not ban cyclamates, but I'm just pointing out that these are the things which tend to control individuals, these outer things. And still we are inclined to feel that we are so normal, that this is the way life is and we just have to put up with it. But I'm here to tell you that this isn't so, that this isn't the way life is; this merely gives indication that we aren't aligned with life.

Now, you recall last week I mentioned that life comes to focus in individuals and expresses out into the environment. The question is: How do we utilize this life which comes to focus in us? We noted that we have the body, the mind and what we call the spiritual expression, and then out beyond this we have the environment. Now the very first thing which is touched by life is the spirit, so that if we are really to know life, to enjoy life, to express the beauty of life, then our spirit, our attitudes, need to be attuned with life. In other words, they need to reveal the characteristics of life itself. So, first we feel something, sense something; then we begin to have a thought in relationship to it; and the thought is the forerunner to the action which takes place through the body — maybe we do something with our hands.

Now the question we need to ask is, How are our capacities used? Are they used for life's purposes or are they used for our own individual purposes? This is something we really need to look at because it is this, actually, which gives us the answers as to whether there is going to be any light at the end of the tunnel. In other words if that which is finding expression through our capacities is of the nature of what we call wrong spirits then we find there is going to be destruction on every hand. Now you might say, 'Well, I wouldn't entertain any wrong spirits!' Oh, you wouldn't? You wouldn't entertain such spirits as resentment? Did you ever resent anybody? What about greed? Everybody seems to a large extent to operate on the basis of 'I want,' don't they? 'I want this and I want that.' I had a gentleman write to me the other day. He said, 'I never could really understand this business of not wanting. I stopped to consider why it was I was always wanting. Suddenly I realized that I had not really been taught anything else from the time I was a babe.' For example, one of the first questions was, 'What do you want to be when you grow up?' Well, what do you want? Do you want to express that which is in alignment with life? Or is the wanting and desire of your heart toward something that is going to be pleasing to you? Unless we're actually aligned with life, letting that particular spirit find expression through us, our wants are going to be those that are pleasing to ourselves, and this separates us from life. So we could say that from the time we are born we are more or less on death row.

Someone handed me a letter which some young person had sent in to a magazine. It revealed something of the attitude which we need to have. This particular article was headed, 'Love of Life,' and she deals with some of the things we have already talked about this evening. 'Vietnam, gun control, student demonstrations, race riots, a Republican President and a Democratic Congress are all explosive issues of today. Right now someone somewhere is complaining, taking sides. Well, I am taking sides, too. I am taking the side of life.' Now what this reveals is that we have a choice, that we can choose to let all of these other things govern our lives or we can choose to take the side of life; and when we do we begin to live. When we say these things we aren't saying that Vietnam isn't a fact, that the riots are not a fact and we will just ignore them. No. What we are saying is that the only answer to these things is that you and I express the true characteristics of life. When we do this we begin to see the nothingness of these other things. We see, for instance, that war, the riots, are merely the absence of peace. If you have peace, can you have war at the same time? If you have been at peace within yourself, do you at the same time feel conflict? No, you can't have both at the same time. If we find, for instance, that you and your friend have had a conflict of some kind, what is going to allow something to resolve the situation? As long as the attitude is 'I can't stand that person; look what he did to me!' there is going to be conflict. But the moment there is a shift in consciousness and we begin to recognize the beauty of expression in that other person the conflict is gone and we find there is peace and harmony between the two again. It is really a state of consciousness, isn't it? So how needful that we begin to recognize that in all of these situations in which we find ourselves we have the responsibility of letting the right expression be present so what is needful can come into that situation. This is vital. But the problem is that individuals do not want to take that responsibility. Now here is a young girl who indicates that she does: 'I am taking the side of life.' And if she actually does then she is saying, 'I can do something about the situation which is in the world.'

She goes on to ask whether we've looked at the mountains, the sunrise, and so forth. We tend to turn toward nature to find some solace because we recognize that nature, when allowed to do so, reveals true beauty, it reveals the reality of itself. These beautiful flowers here, they are just being what they are. They are revealing something beautiful. This evening I noted the sky was very beautiful, and I remarked on it to my friend as we were walking along together. The clouds with the reflection of the sun on them allowed something very beautiful to be known. How important that we begin to reflect, as it were, the reality of ourselves through our capacities so that the beauty of ourselves is seen, and likewise the beauty of others. You know, if we really look we can see the beauty of others. I look at you here and I see the beauty. It is not because you are all smiling or that you have to do this or that to make me recognize the beauty, but there is the awareness that in you there is the reality of life which allows a true beauty of expression to be known. And so, as we are gathered here, as we actually come in oneness to share something together, we may provide something that can be described as beautiful, exquisite. Look at the group of flowers there. Just one of them is beautiful, but see how lovely an arrangement like that is. We have an arrangement here tonight, don't we? And I love this arrangement. And because each one of us begins to love the situation in which we find ourselves, to recognize that life in all of us is one thing, we appreciate each other. We appreciate what is here and recognize the true beauty that is present with us.

And so this girl was looking at the mountains and she saw this. She said, 'Stop! When was the last time you watched an ant, heard a bird sing, smelled a wildflower, felt the cool freshness of a mountain stream or tasted the salt mist of an ocean breeze? When was the last time you simply said, "Life is beautiful. I'm glad that I am a part of it." ' Are you glad you are a part of life? You are alive, aren't you, so you can say, 'I am life.' We recall that these were words which Jesus spoke many years ago. He said, 'I am the way, the truth, and the life.' 'I am come that they might have life, and that they might have it more abundantly.' So if we are a part of life, well that's the reason we are here, that we can actually express the reality of life.

Some of you will recall, in an earlier talk, that I had a magnetic man here. We had a group of magnets in a certain formation representing that which you really are. And we put iron filings on the paper surface, behind which were these magnets, so that the filings were drawn into the shape of a man, showing the arms, the legs, the body and so forth. And we noted that life, being what we really are, is well able to draw together this physical form, and that if the form is to be maintained it must continue to be aligned with life itself. The moment that this alignment with life is interfered with in any way we find there is a pattern of disintegration which begins to take place in the body. I mention this because we referred to the matter of anger; someone becomes very angry. And we know that when we are angry – I'm sure we've all experienced it – something has taken place in our body chemistry so that we just don't feel like eating. We don't feel we really want to be with anybody – unless they are angry about the same thing; then we sort of come together. But in any case, I had cards labeled as various wrong attitudes, which I put between the magnets and the iron filings. And as these cards were placed between we found that gradually the iron filings began to fall away. Well this is actually what happens to our individual bodies, because when we are controlled by anger, and all these other feelings, we are actually going through the process of disintegration. We call the final thing death, but there is this gradual pattern of dying which is taking place all the time.

Now, the effects of these things on the body have been proven out in the laboratory. Air has been passed through iced tubes; people have breathed through them and the breath condenses as it goes through the tube. They have found that if a person is angry or resentful, or expresses any of the other destructive characteristics, the condensation has a color to it. I'm not going to say that it is green with envy, or red with anger, but it does have a color to it. And they have also found that there is a definite change in the chemical structure of the cells; so that man is slowly committing suicide by being aligned with these attitudes. And still he seems to think that this is the way. But as I indicated earlier, this is not the way to get out of the tunnel. We find that it is only in actual alignment with life that something begins to move in essence through us which allows us to come out of the tunnel.

And so as we come together in these gatherings my deepest concern is to help you to realize that there is an answer and that you are the answer. You and I are the answer whereby these so-called problems can be solved. The only real problem is that we are no longer really aligned with life. Aligning ourselves with life we find that changes begin to take place in and through us.

Now, those of you who were here last time recall that we shared a portion of the book *As of a Trumpet*, and I think perhaps the words in there say a little more specifically what I would convey this evening. Here is a further passage from this book:

> The paths of men are dark and devious. Some walk deliberately in them, others ignorantly. There is a straight path and a right way. Those who long to find it shall hear my voice.

The voice of life, of love, of truth.

> The Lord of whom I speak is not the figurehead of religious belief nor mere invention of vain imagination. The word may be rightly translated as Jehovah and it simply means, God in action on earth.

This is what I have been talking to you about tonight. You will recall, those of you that know your Bible, that there was reference made to the fact that the people knew Him as God Almighty, but

as Jehovah they knew Him not; in other words even today we think
of the Lord, or God, as something far off, as God Almighty, but
we haven't come to know Him as God in action through men and
women. And so this is what we are talking about here. Now, as I
emphasized last week, let's not get hung up on the words *God* and
Lord, and so forth; let's not let our religious concepts of what we
think these words mean get in the way of our understanding of
what we are really talking about.

> Prepare ye the way for divine action on earth. God acts
> through man.

How else?

> Therefore I am come to prepare men to let God act, that His
> creative path may be made straight.
> My voice sounds in the earthly wilderness which is the
> tangled man-made world.

Man-made, you notice.

> Let all with ears to hear hearken to my word and to the living
> spirit which is the substance of it. Come near unto me.

This is the word of life which we are speaking about here, which
comes and is spoken, and to which we are asked to draw near.

> To you who hear I speak, calling many things to your re-
> membrance. Some of what I say you may think you already
> know. Have patience. With other things you may not agree.
> Withhold your judgment.
> Your true nature is divine, not merely human. This indi-
> cates a quality of character which is transcendent. This tran-
> scendent character is an already existing potential.

It is already there; it is life.

> Some of this potential may have been partially realized, but
> there is as yet vastly more unknown to you than known. When
> known this is the truth that makes you free.
> The reality indicated by the word *God* includes this truth

of your own divine nature. Your acquaintance therefore with God can be no more than your acquaintance with yourSelf as you divinely are.

Now, that 'Self' has a capital 'S' – 'with yourSelf as you divinely are.'

Some believe and some deny the existence of God. In either case acceptance or rejection is based in the idea of what the word means to those concerned, or perhaps the attitude may be inherited without thought.

That is true, isn't it? How many just inherit the attitude which they might have toward God from their parents, without thought!

When the idea is of a logical nature no doubt acceptance will be compelled. Likewise with an unreasonable concept intelligence and honesty require rejection. However the word *God* may be used to define a reality which is capable of being known to the extent that you come to know your true Self. Neither belief nor unbelief is necessary when the truth is known.

If you are to know your Self, you must first admit that the self which you know is at best but a hint of your true Self. It is unlikely that the experience of identity you have known has always been characterized by the highest vision then possible to you, let alone by the divine state yet beyond your awareness. Who without self-righteousness can claim to be all that he inherently knows he could be?

Your consciousness of present identity is likely to be closely associated with your physical body. Various mental and emotional characteristics and idiosyncrasies are also included in the personality which you think yourself to be. All these elements, constituting your human nature, are derived from hereditary sources and environmental experiences. Consequently you are conscious of a self which is merely a conglomerate amalgam stemming from the myriad influences out of your historical past, combined with the reactions induced by them.

However this composite self of which you are aware cannot be you who are aware of it.

The observer can't observe himself, is what is being said.

Neither is it a true revelation of you. It is rather the reflection of an unnatural state brought to you out of the past, resulting from the experience of countless generations of people who lacked any real awareness of divine identity. This is not you nor does it give evidence of the real nature of your true Self.

You are divine. You are not the conglomerate self-made self. However you are also human which fact makes it possible for your divine Self to be experienced and made known on earth.

Inherently in you are all the essences of your divinely individual character. You are the potential of the divine revelation of yourSelf on earth. When you are your true Self on earth, God is in action on earth because of you. Insofar as you personally are concerned the way of the Lord has then been prepared and His paths made straight.

We said earlier we are life: 'I am a part of life.' Therefore the true Self finds expression through the human capacities of body, mind and spiritual expression, and this in truth is God in action on earth – not something mysterious but something which each one can know and experience for himself. When we actually come to know ourselves we find that we are in position to let the light shine at the end of the tunnel. It can't shine until you know yourself, that's the truth of the matter. And so our concern is to assist all to come to an awareness of Self so that there can be the true expression of life here on earth. It is not going to be found through what President Nixon, the newspapers, or anybody else says, until there is the true expression through individual human beings. There may be things with which you do not agree. Hold your judgment. Begin to experience in your own living that which I have been talking about; begin to experience oneness with life.

It is only when there is the right expression through us as individuals that we can know what it is to be one. People are looking for this, aren't they, and they say, in theory, 'We're all one. There must be integration.' Yet our very actions say we are separate. Our so-called minority groups say, 'We are separate but we are going to force ourselves to be one, to be included in this larger whole.' But you can never force yourself in any way whatsoever to be one, because in reality you are already one. So we come to recognize something of the reality of our oneness as each one begins to express what is true of him- or herself. Then it is one, because life is one thing.

So I'm going to leave you with these thoughts and we will find that, if some of these points don't seem to be understandable, they will be clarified. But basically there needs to be an expression of life through us which actually says, 'Here is the light! I am the light! Come near unto me!' And we find that in knowing the truth of this, in oneness, there is a great light, there is a great beauty.

A talk given at Free University, Sunrise Ranch, Loveland, Colorado, November 3, 1969.

ROGER DE WINTON was born in England but has spent his adult years in Canada and the United States. He was an officer in the Royal Canadian Navy during World War II and had extensive business experience, specifically in banking.

He has for some twenty years now played a central part in the unfoldment of the community known as Sunrise Ranch and also the much larger form of the worldwide Emissary family.

His prime concern has been with the health of this emerging form from a spiritual standpoint, and the practical nature of this approach as it affects the body, mind and emotional realms of people.

THE INVISIBLE DRIVER

Roger de Winton

We, with millions of others, have been living largely on the surface, never really discovering our true selves. I suppose most of us have gotten sick of this and so we are searching for something new, something different. The search is for our own true expression. In order to do this we are moving through a little book which I have in my hand, entitled *As of a Trumpet*, which is a kind of primer on what you might call discovering yourself step by step. If you are willing to take this book and read it with your heart open, and are willing to work through the steps suggested in this book, you will find a new expression, because the one who wrote the book has already done this. So we are actually following the results of experience. So here we go.

'Your divine nature is unique.' Okay. Do you believe that? Look at one another. Do you think you are all the same? No. Obviously everybody in this room is unique, even on the surface, let alone what is underneath. So this we can see is true even as we start.

Your divine nature is unique. As the specific differentiation of love, which is your true nature, in turn is differentiated in the unique expression of your Self on earth, this is the divine state for you.

The translation of your divine potential into the actual experience of this state occurs as your love for God exceeds all other emotional involvements. It is the real fact in this regard, not the mere desire, that counts.

The principle of focalization applies to your love for God. The manner of its application must be understood and accepted if the divine state is to be known by you. The right application draws your response in love toward the one at the apex of this system, in whom all the differentiations of love within the system come to focus. He is the Lord your God. Regardless of the name used to identify Him, He is the focalization of God for you.

Maybe we have gone far enough; better do something with it. Let's go back to what we've just said. 'The one at the apex of this system, in whom all the differentiations of love within the system come to focus. He is the Lord your God.' All right, let's say that this cross represents the Lord our God. There are something over four billion people on earth, only 204 million in the United States, but four billion on earth. However, we'll just indicate two of them on the board with x's. Now here we are; this is us. One of these is us, and we are connected up to the Lord our God. Now let us say

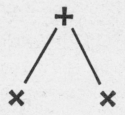

these two people, as we have seen, are just like snowflakes, always different; they are never stamped out the same. Therefore if this one over here is connected with the Lord and that one over there is connected with the Lord, and they are different, then what they actually are is love – which the Lord is – differentiated out here as a person, as a being if you like. We'll start off by recognizing that there is a beautiful, perfect, real self within this outer cover, which built this outer cover, built this heart and mind over a period of years. And this one is still within. So we could, I suppose, forget the outer circle altogether and say that there are actually on earth today four-billion-plus beings perfectly connected up in love with the Lord their God. And these perfect beings actually allow, con-

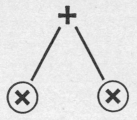

stantly, a differentiation of this love to appear as far as it is possible for them through the outer cover. So we draw the outer cover. Unfortunately, due to the consciousness of what you might call the little self, or the outer person, there is so little awareness of the fact that the unseen driver in the seat is perfect and perfectly connected up with this God that there is a comparative distortion, to put it mildly, in our outer cover, not only in the outer cover of the physique but also in the outer covering of the heart and mind, so that we have one hang of a mess on earth. But if we can bring ourselves with open hearts for a moment to consider this, we can see how that love goes down the connection – whatever it is – from this center out to each of these and is characterized out in an individual sense from there.

This may be very strange and very new and all the rest, but as we remain open to this consideration perhaps something may start to percolate, may start to come into our remembrance a little, so that while a word may seem a little strange, the feeling which we have concerning such a connection may not be so strange at all, provided that we don't insist on trying to analyze it with our brilliant minds. The main thing in this session is to take a chance, to let go a little to the possibilities of something absolutely marvelous, far beyond the miniscule comprehension of our minds. Unless I am willing in this moment to let go to an awareness which is far greater than my mind I couldn't possibly speak the way I am. The whole thing would make no sense at all. So here we have the acorn, as you might say, of love. And out here millions and millions – it would be a tremendous oak tree – of branches, each differentiating in its own beautiful, special way the essential core of the acorn which provides the initial beginning of the oak tree, a reasonable analogy.

> He is the Lord your God. Regardless of the name used to identify Him, He is the focalization of God for you. Your love for Him and for the fulness of the divine nature focalized by Him and differentiated through you and others, must be complete. When it is, nothing other than the pure expression of your own divine nature could ever find release through your thoughts, feelings, words and deeds.
>
> Your love for this supreme one is at the same time your love for your true Self.

Well, of course. If you have, to start with, a sort of theoretical love, you know, a miniscule awareness of love for the moment, but at least something, a starting point, a feeling, a beginning reminder of something great which stands behind you and me, then obviously there is a beginning appreciation for what you might call the unseen driver which stands behind the outer cover. We go to bed at night and somehow we are carried through the night by the unseen driver, and we wake up in the morning and the unseen driver is apparently still carrying on – hearts are beating, minds are awake, all the rest, the whole thing in operation. And yet we, brilliant people on the surface, haven't the vaguest idea how it is all done. So presumably, on this basis, we should have a very good appreciation for the real driver, standing in the invisible seat there and beautifully connected, maintaining this beautiful connection and understanding with the Lord his God or her God, unseen also and yet very much in operation.

'Your love for this supreme one is at the same time your love for your true Self and also your love for your neighbor.' Well, of course, if we come to this awareness that there is an unseen driver in me, well then presumably I am sufficiently unselfcentered to recognize that there is an unseen driver in you. And therefore I start to appreciate you not so much as the outer cover, or the personality – that you don't like so much: 'He blows in his soup' . . . all these other things that people don't like, all these surface things – but one comes to marvel at the wonderful way in which the unseen one has built and maintained one's neighbor. This also may be a little theoretical for a while, but it is all right, because as one starts to appreciate, and continues to appreciate, the central one and one's own unseen driver, then presumably this will set something in motion which will bring a deeper appreciation for others. There is a lot of nonsense spoken, isn't there, about 'I love everyone.' I've often wondered what these people who say 'I love everyone' really mean. I think it is probably just a feeling of the moment, possibly of the hour, possibly for a whole evening. But when they wake up in the dawn and they see some of the other people around that they haven't seen for a while, they may not love everyone in quite the same way. Have you had that experience? So the appreciation then needs to be for the unseen neighbor, who has a very beautiful exterior or otherwise. This is what the appreciation is for, isn't it?

'For all the differentiated aspects of the divine nature within this system are contained in essence at the apex point of focus.' Well of course, because if love is the character of the central essence and this love is the character of the unseen driver, then the central essence must contain love. And everybody else is basically seasoned, shall we say, essenced in love. No matter what goes on on the surface, this is what is really there. 'The system is one. In it there is one identity, focalized at the apex and differentiated into individual aspects throughout. Thus is the system composed.' Four billion beings with outer covers presently marching the earth; maybe rebellious outer covers, as we know, very unwilling outer covers, but nevertheless they are on earth and in operation.

'This system is the potential for a corresponding system, or "body," in form on earth.' All right, let's take one more look. We've got four billion of these unseen drivers. They certainly form a body, they really know what it is all about, they really have a purpose, and they have four billion outer covers who haven't the vaguest idea what the purpose is and are mostly operating on their own individual wants. This is a very tough way of looking at it, but of course you and I aren't involved! We can say, 'Those people out there, you see. It is the other 3,999,999,960!' But, in any case, there they are, these other covers, flitting around with their own purposes – which change, as we have noted, from time to time, don't they? And yet within these are the representatives of the four billion bodies unseen.

'This system is the potential for a corresponding system, or "body," in form on earth.' Okay. When the outer covers start to behave themselves then we have the beginnings of a possible four-billion family on earth, working together. I think that takes more imagination than the beginning part of this talk, at the moment. 'When the potential is fully realized the earthly "body" is a revelation of the divine system. This is God in action on earth.' That's all right, isn't it? When you have four billion people on earth, or however many, who are willing to participate in this, who are allowing the character of love to come forth through the outer cover consistently in all their doings, then you have the revelation of this essence at the apex point, coming down through into the unseen driver, coming out through the unseen driver at last into the earth and blessing whatever the world is, the particular personal world to start with, that surrounds this person. Because, as was pointed out, we each center our own world; whatever lies in your environment, under your hand of responsibility, is your world. It isn't necessarily completely in this city, is it? It may extend far away.

So there is this need, then, for the family to start to develop: love initiated here, differentiated, in other words, brought forth uniquely by the unseen driver who is the real us, into our environment. And as the unseen driver takes control much comes into consciousness which has never been there before; much of our responsibility, much of the joy of sharing love of life with others and of opening up, perhaps, relationships with people whom we have thought hardly worth considering, etc., etc. And our world, which has been waiting for us, starts to get the attention which it should have. And so you have what I quoted: '... the potential for a corresponding system, or "body," in form on earth. When the potential is fully realized the earthly "body" is a revelation of the divine system. This is God in action on earth.'

'The way by which this occurs is the creative process. In the unfoldment of it there is a further differentiation of the divine nature through the manifest system or "body" into the larger environment.' This is what I've just been talking about, isn't it? In other words we start to become aware of our worlds, worlds beyond immediate family, beyond just the job, beyond a few contacts or whatever, into something much larger. Perhaps that seems almost staggering at the moment, but here we go anyway. 'Thus the animal, vegetable and mineral kingdoms begin to give increasing evidence of the divine state in expanded expression.' Well this is something I guess we all know. For instance, there are many people on earth who have what is called 'a green thumb.' Such people don't forget to water their plants and they don't water them too much. Such people give love. They have a tremendous appreciation for these living things. And because of this appreciation and the necessary loving attention, something tremendous happens. They call it a green thumb. And yet something tremendous happens through that person at that level. And this of course is only a miniscule part of such a person's world, actually. However, even that is a beautiful thing to see. Some people say that they love animals more than people. And dogs that want to bite others come and play with them because they feel this beautiful unseen driver moving through the outer capacities, and the dog, having a natural response to the unseen driver, just leaps for joy; it is easy. So here we see something of the divine nature, which we call it here; the kingdom coming at another level. This is great. 'So does the kingdom of heaven which is at hand, merely potential, come on earth in actual form and function.

'The reproduction of the divine system in manifest form necessarily reveals the principle of focalization in operation on earth.' Okay. In other words, once the unseen driver starts to come forth through one outer cover, and the unseen driver starts to come forth through another, and they are both in agreement with the central point – with God – because they both reveal His character, love, in their own particular way on earth, then it is obvious that they aren't just two people wandering around with their own particular desires and purposes and shortsightedness and all the rest. And something starts to happen, because, obviously, if God has His own character in expression through people, those people are going to be in agreement, because their character is the same and their central point of control is in God and they know it. That is what we've got to come to know, isn't it? 'The working of this principle, being inherent in the design of the divine system, cannot be established by the determinations of the unreal self without distorting it.'

There is the tough one. Let me read that again, 'The working of this principle, being inherent in the design of the divine system' – in other words, the system with all the people in it, with all the invisible drivers in it – 'cannot be established by the determinations of the unreal self without distorting it. As long as the unreal self is present and active the true design will be obscured.' In other words I have suggested, in the leadup to this, that once you have the unseen drivers moving through their outer capacities, allowing a beautiful understanding of love and the understanding of the system to be in movement out in the outer earth – to the plants, to the people, to the whole thing – then it becomes apparent that there is an agreement, that there is a coherence, a cohesiveness, among people. And then of course we – not us, but some others – who got left behind in this deal and are still operating on the basis of 'I want my way, I've got an idea that what I'd really like to do is something over here today which will suit me, which will give me enjoyment and satisfaction,' and so on, we look at this which is going on and we say, 'Well how can we fit into this game? These people are obviously having some success here. Let's see, how can we get into this? How can we have our fun, have our little short-sighted couple of years, ten-year projects, whatever, and still get into this league?' You can't, because these people, these invisible drivers with their outer covers moving rightly, know what they are up to, they know the way they are going. And they are not the slightest bit interested anymore in one-year, two-year, three-year projects; they are interested in a purpose that is divine, and which is, incidentally, eternal. As we have long since come to discover, the purpose initially of the members of such a body emerging on earth is first of all to completely emerge in consciousness themselves, so that they have their capacities clear, and then to assist many others to come to the same awareness so that their invisible drivers may come into the driver's seat and start to move in this same purpose. Well of course this has absolutely nothing to do with the kind of things that you and I have been involved with: build a house, a couple of cars, child, the whole bit – it sounds very good. Well, I mean, really . . . these may come, of course, in the divine nature and design of life, but it isn't the purpose. Of course, I'm sure some of us in this room have had very lofty purposes, far beyond what I am saying, but you know that many of the four billion that I am speaking of fell for these kinds of purposes.

So here we are, then, with two lots: We have those who are calling to people in their sickbed to wake up, having got their facilities in hand, so that they too may come to an awareness of what we are starting to do in life. Then you have the others around, saying, 'This looks like a good thing; let's get on the bandwagon,' without realizing what bandwagon they are getting onto. And when they start to bring their little shortsighted ideas, what they want to do in their lives, and try to bring them into the system, it certainly doesn't work. And this is the point at which some of us found ourselves.

As long as the unreal self is present and active the true design will be obscured. Consequently only the willingness of the unreal self to lose its life for the sake of your real Self, permits the design of the divine system to take form on earth.

The whole creative fulfilment is dependent, therefore, upon the correct individual choice. Insofar as you are concerned it is dependent upon the extent to which your unreal self will release you into the experience of your real Self on earth. The unreal self must decrease, the real Self increase.

'Your Self' is what I have called the unseen driver. Now, we'll get into this a little further, but just at this moment let us look at what we have been doing. We have found that for the unreal self to decrease and for the real self to increase, basically we need to be consciously on the alert to do to the highest of our vision in every moment. Now you say, 'It sounds awfully dull – do the right thing

– like the Boy Scouts or something.' But as we insist upon our choice being right rather than any old thing we'd like, then we find that there is a chain of events starting to take place.

First of all we find that, for instance, our lives are no longer quite as uncertain as they have been. Have you found sometimes that your days are a little uncertain, a little uncertain as to how events are going to work out, and whether one is going to be reasonably successful in these events? And yet, as we make a point of deliberately making a right choice, we find more and more that, for one thing, things start to work out, things appear to be relatively under control. And, of course, we start to have a new assurance. You have to be careful that it isn't a new assurance in this human ego. But we start to have a new assurance that when we move out into a day, even though the most seemingly terrible things come up, we are capable of maintaining a right attitude, an intelligent, interested, patient attitude, so that this real driver which stands behind, which is us, may have the opportunity of working step by step through this apparently terrible thing. Now, I think, as many of us have discovered, in points of crisis we do allow this to happen. It is remarkable how different the outcome is; it is not the usual surface expectation. Now, many of us know this already. So this is a very down-to-earth thing we are dealing with: the need for making a right choice and continuing to make it, not being on-again, off-again; or it doesn't work.

If you wish to correlate all that I have been saying to you with the recorded words and actions of Jesus Christ, you will discover that I am calling them to your remembrance. I do not invite you to accept some strange belief according to the doctrines of the unreal self, but show you the way, the truth and the life by which your divine Self may come on earth here and now.

So we are interested in the expression of our divine, unique nature. And we are starting to see that as our interest lies in allowing the character of love to be ours in expression, that then, even though we can't go inside and find the unseen driver who has built us from one cell to this present point and maintained us, we may still so cooperate with that unseen driver that the outer self and the inner self merge and we come to know ourselves in expression. We can never dig in and find the unseen driver; it simply cannot be done. But we can know our own expression, and that is just perfect, just lovely; that is all that is needed.

So, then, the first step in the release of this unseen driver is the determination to maintain an attitude of right choice. It isn't a gritting-of-the-teeth situation; it is something which is going to be enjoyable but in a different way from what we have known to date. If we are going at this purely so that we may have enjoyment on another basis, well what is the difference from the old guy which we have previously been? He is going to have his enjoyment and, incidentally, this Lord our God is going to get a good servant on earth; it is all going to be a good deal. We're taking God into partnership, silent partnership, and it will all be great and everything will be fine, etc. No! No! It just won't work. There is the Lord our God; there is this One who has allowed these unseen drivers to come to earth, to surround themselves with outer covers, ready to do a job. We cannot reach inside to our unseen driver. We are tremendously blessed therefore that we can devote our loving attention to this unseen One, this God. And because our unseen driver is already in agreement with Him, then the driver and the outer cover are together. That makes the whole thing possible.

As this driver is already bringing forth that which is right and beautiful and fitting, then because we are interested in bringing forth that which is right and beautiful and fitting and responsible we are together as one, and the driver starts to emerge. Well why should this driver be doing things that are right, fitting and responsible? Because love's characteristics are right, fitting and responsible.

We will find that in this business of wishing to be right, one of the first things we come against is being honest. We perhaps have had a certain surface honesty which, when we start to move on the basis of real honesty, we are amazed to realize how surfacy it really is. This experience of insisting upon being right and being honest starts to deepen our awareness in events. Many decisions which perhaps we would have made with a flip of the fingers are not made that way anymore. This doesn't mean that we retire to our chambers at least a dozen times a day to give deep consideration to what is right, because we shall find, as we are interested in being right, that instead of moving on the basis of two factors drawn into consciousness, we shall find that our growing perception will automatically draw many more factors into consciousness.

And what happens? Our environment, instead of being visited by what you might call a curse, in other words a surface person who hardly knows what he or she is doing, starts to be blessed with the power of a thoughtful, right person in expression. I think it was not long ago that I was dealing with something like this in one of these sessions. And I suggested that probably most of us in the room had been through the experience where we had come slap up against a wall in our lives and needed some counseling; we needed to go and talk to somebody. Now, I would think for many of us that this wouldn't necessarily mean we would talk to somebody in our family – it's odd but it is true. I think for many of us this meant that we would go and pick somebody who we felt had the goods, somebody who would be willing to consider our problem as we thought of it and listen to our story, and allow sufficient of the factors which were needed to come into his or her consciousness so that what we shared would be to our advantage. We have already, many of us, been aware that there are those on earth, even in the outer man's sense, who to a degree are sound people. And they are sound because to a degree they are allowing something of this to happen without realizing that they are part of the God family. There are very few people on earth who are aware that they are a part of the God family, really. I think if you went amongst your acquaintances and said what I have said tonight you'd have a hang of a job selling it. So if this is true of some who are unknowingly allowing this particular process to take place, how much more true it should be of you and me who are becoming aware of the fact that when you allow the right characteristics of honesty, etc., to be yours and mine, then automatically you start to awaken. Your perception starts to open up to the factors which are needed to take the action which is needed, and we get on the road – we start to move. The marvelous thing about this is that we find that there is a seemingly unseen power moving in our lives which allows many factors to come into the situation which would have never been normally thought of.

Now, you'll have to try it out to find out. But this is the fact. In the divine setup it isn't a case of adding one and one and making two. Both in the case of unseen drivers and in the case of dealing with situations, you will find that it is a multiplication business we are in. Things multiply very quickly, so that, provided we maintain this attitude of rightness and the desire to be fitting, the power of God starts to move effectively into our environment and we are then a blessing far greater than simply an ordinary human being endeavoring to do the right thing. It is a quite different experience.

We have talked about power. Let's go back to this individual and collective business. If, let us say, you undertake some action out here as one individual, how much power do you think you have moving? Practically nothing, do you? You say, 'I'll go and do it.' Great! Many of us have put our feet in our mouths doing that. And yet, as we allow ourselves to be divinely drawn together because we wish to be right, we wish to align ourselves with the character here, this loving character, then the factors come to consciousness. Our perception of events, of people, everything, starts to open up and we start to come out of this absurd case, this shell we've been stuck in. We become what you might call resilient people, physically too, but particularly at other levels. Did you ever see a person who was old and afraid, walking alone, no trust in God, no trust in anything but what is left of them on the surface? All right, we don't want that; we need this other thing.

So here we are with these factors being drawn together. But I think into our consciousness must come the immense responsibility which we carry. If I am simply speaking to you of techniques – 'Be right and allow the factors to come through and all will be well' – and we have no awakening vision of our own individual worlds for which we are already responsible, which is far greater than we recognize at this stage, then how long do you think we are going to keep going? I don't think very long. I think we could sell out fairly easily. 'You know, the opening, the little opening of perception, a little greater awareness, events around me working out rather

well, my whole life is starting to move. I'm having a great time!'
Me! Me! Me! Me! Me! Me! *ME!* But how great a vision do
you think that is for a person who is allowing the unseen driver,
who is already aware that there is a tremendous job to be done on
earth in the awakening of his own facilities, and then the drawing
back into place of whatever of the human race will come? That's
the job! And so, while we may for the moment live in the sun,
enjoy the development of our capacities and find that life is working out better as we do the fitting thing, let's not sell out for that
miniscule vision. Let us be alert to the fact that any of us who
become aware of what I have been speaking of, and of the possibilities of what may be given into our environment as we do the
right thing, have a far greater job than we have any awareness of
at the present time. You may not have a vision that reaches out to
it completely, but it doesn't matter. What matters is that there is
this unseen driver in us that is starting to gather his or her strength
from within these capacities. And as we allow a greater vision,
then perhaps we can momentarily see it, even though for the
moment largely as theory. Nevertheless we shall keep going, without thinking that we've got years to do it. We shall keep going to
allow great changes to come in our experience fairly swiftly.

A talk given at Free University, Sunrise Ranch, Loveland, Colorado, November 30, 1970 .

DR. WILLIAM BAHAN is a native of New Hampshire and for many years, together with his brother Walter, developed the largest non-medical health clinic in North America. Dr. Bahan's keen insight into the need for health for the whole man has been the theme of his work over the years.

He was coordinator of the faculty at the Emissary Servers Training School in Loveland, Colorado, for nine years, before developing Emissary educational facilities and courses in the eastern and southern states. He is a worldwide lecturer and is providing an increasingly significant point of leadership for those seeking the truth of themselves in many countries the world around.

THE WAY TO THE WAY OF LIFE

William Bahan

It would seem that human beings have lost their way. There are very few on earth today who can say in fact, 'Life is terrific; I'm having a most wonderful experience.' Few there are who find that, and few there are who are having that experience. If people aren't having an experience, a continuous, creative experience, an experience where they may say consistently, 'Life is terrific,' it isn't because it is life's fault. It is because they are not in the way of life; they've gotten out of the way.

The greatest art is the art of living. We have become very proficient at the art of dying; we know very little, seemingly, about living. It does seem strange that we shouldn't know very much about living, because what could be closer to us than life? – nearer than breathing and closer than hands and feet. We say, 'I have life.' You say to someone, 'You have it? What is it?' 'I don't know.' Here we have it and don't know what it is! Maybe the reason we don't know what it is is because we ain't what we is. Maybe when we is what we really is we'll find out what life is. I think that we could get quick agreement on the fact that human beings are not very proficient at living, because, as I say, if one is in fact living he is having a creative experience. It has nothing to do with environment. Of all the nonsense that human beings have thought up, the most ridiculous is to blame their environment for their experience. 'Oh, I'm unhappy because of this; I'm depressed; I'm sad.' You're a phony! Your environment has nothing to do with it. When you clear that in consciousness you take a big step in the right direction. If you're not having that creative experience it has nothing to do with your environment. Anyone who says it does does so because they are not having a creative experience and they want to blame their environment.

I have a little book here, the *Bhagavad-gita*. It is some Indian
literature that maybe many of you have read, probably heard
about. It is also called *The Song Celestial*. Most beautiful literature, many, many, many thousands of years old. It was taken from
the Sanskrit. I mention the age of it because they were having the
same problem then as we are having now. There is no improve-
ment. Nothing has changed 'since the fathers fell asleep.' Everything has seemingly remained the same. By the way, contained in
this book is also the solution to those problems, but no one sees
that. They miss the solutions. So I thought tonight, as a starting
point for our consideration, I might just read a portion of *The
Song Celestial* to you. In the book, just to clue some of those who
have no background of the story, there are many characters, but
the two major characters are Arjuna and Krishna. They represent
something in symbolical language. Krishna represents the inner
reality of being and Arjuna represents the outer man and, more
particularly, the capacity for spiritual expression which man has.
Now in the story there is a conversation taking place between
Arjuna and Krishna, and it is very unusual because Arjuna is
listening to Krishna; the outer self is listening to the inner self.
Most people don't realize that they have this reality of being that
is contained within. There is a Krishna. This aspect of the cosmic
All That Is is contained in each person, and very few even recognize it. In this story Arjuna, the outer self, is listening to the inner
self, and asks the inner self a question in this portion I'm going to
read to you. Listen to the question; it's loaded.

> ARJUNA: Yet tell me, Teacher! by what force doth man
> Go along his way, unwilling; as if one
> Pushed him that troubled path?

Good question! What is the force that is pushing human beings
around? – and where in the world are the human beings who aren't
being pushed around? Where are those who, as I mentioned earlier, are leading and having a continuous creative experience?
Where are the human beings that aren't unhappy, depressed, frustrated, and blaming their environment for this lousy experience?
So, Arjuna wanted to know. He said, 'What's this force that is

pushing man down the troubled path?' Listen to what Krishna said:

KRISHNA: Life it is!
Life's urge it is! used in darkened understanding,
Which pusheth him. Mighty of appetite,
Powerful, and strong is this! – man's enemy or friend!

Ah, that's the right answer I would say, wouldn't you? 'Life it is!' And he said it is used in darkened understanding. Isn't that beautifully put? This is the problem of course. We have life and we have been seeking to use life, but with darkened understanding. If we seek to use life with darkened understanding, as Krishna mentioned, we will find that life is an enemy. Not that it is life's fault. How many times have you seen tragedies and unhappy situations, people sick? And people say, 'Oh that's life, you know.' They always attribute something horrible to life. No, that isn't life. If we see tragedy, if we see sadness and suffering, it isn't life's fault. It is what Krishna says here, 'Life . . . used in darkened understanding'; that's the problem. Once we begin to allow life to have its way with us we find that life is a friend. Do you always find, every hour of every day, that life is your friend? Or do you say, 'Ah to hell with it!'? Do you ever get depressed, ever get discouraged? By the way, you should be thankful if you have those experiences, because the fact that you have them shows that you have life. The moment we have no life . . . corpses aren't depressed or unhappy. Isn't it interesting with human beings – when they think of peace, what do they think of? Death, don't they? 'God rest his soul, he's finally reached peace,' meaning he's finally stopped being an enemy to life. Now he is having his peace.

How vital it is that we be absolutely sure that we don't seek to use life with darkened understanding. If our understanding is darkened that is what we are trying to do; we are trying to use life. When our understanding begins to clear we begin to find out that it isn't a question of us using life; it is a question of letting life use us. There is a big difference between trying to live life and letting life live you, a big difference, like a navel orange and an orange navel – a big difference. You wouldn't confuse them, would you?

Human beings seeking to use life with darkened understanding have not been very successful. We need to learn to let life use us. But yet, as children we weren't trained to let life use us. We were trained to take life – because this is what our beloved parents were doing – to take life and try to use it, to try to build a design according to our concepts of how this design should be to be pleasing. We haven't succeeded. Even when we are youngsters they are already telling us, 'You should do this, you should do that.' I had an incident last year in New York. A friend of mine, a little girl four or five years old – out of the mouths of babes! – some brilliant human being said to her, 'What do you want to be when you grow up?' She said, 'I be now!' He was saying, in essence, 'Stealing life, what are you going to make it into?' as if life didn't have a design.

This green on this plant is getting a little shabby-looking. But here is the evidence of life's design. Isn't it interesting, whenever you pick up something to portray beauty, have you noticed that we always have to pick the lower forms of creation? – the flowers, the bees, the birds. We never say, 'Here's a beautiful human being.' In order to find beauty we usually have to go to the lower aspects of creation. We don't usually find it in the apex, which man is supposed to be. But here is the evidence of design. Design. My navel is in the right place; it's not under my nose. How come? Who designed that? Life designed it! Now this isn't something that goes along with popular opinion, but life knows what it is doing. Life knows what it is doing. Life has design; life has purpose. We need to learn how to let life live us rather than us trying to live life.

I'm going to read a little more of the *Gita.* Just imagine, this is thousands and thousands of years old and has been lying around all this time and we haven't seen the things that are contained herein. Krishna goes on – the inner reality. Let me just start with this so I can pick up the threads again:

> KRISHNA: Life it is!
> Life's urge it is! used in darkened understanding,
> Which pusheth him. Mighty of appetite,
> Powerful and strong is this! – man's enemy or friend!
> As smoke blots the white fire, as clinging rust

Mars the bright mirror, as the womb surrounds
The babe unborn, so is the world of things
Foiled, soiled, enclosed in wrong uses of Life's Urge.

So we need to learn how to let life have its way with us. Here is a life form, my own, right? Who built it? Well we say, 'Life.' All right. Here is a form of life. You have a form of life or you wouldn't be sitting here tonight. I had a fellow say to me one time, 'Do you think there is life on other planets?' Of all the nonsense! What do you think created that other planet? It's a form, isn't it? It's a life form, and life created *all* things. Life created that planet. Now, what he meant was 'Do you think the forms on other planets are like the forms on earth?' No! The forms on earth are made of earth; the forms on Venus are made of Venus; the forms on Mars are made of Mars. Life uses what is there. It uses the material – whether it is Mars or earth – it uses that to build its forms. So we have earth forms. Life built this, my earth form. We can see the evidence of the design, and we can also see the evidence of control. My hand, if I reach for that flower, doesn't miss it and go beyond. This shows the design to my hand and it also shows control. So, contained within life is design and control, meaning this: that life already has a design for the form; for the forms that are to appear on earth life already has a design.

Now our problem is that we have taken life and started to build our own forms. We have used life in darkened understanding, seeking to build our forms. And of course we all fail. That's one thing I've learned from my relatives: Do exactly the opposite. Have you any relatives that were successful? I look back at my uncle, my aunt, all of my kinsmen. Every one of them was a failure. None of them knew who they were; none of them reached the end of their span on earth and said, 'Man, this has been terrific!' They said they would die and go to heaven, or some such nonsense. None of them knew how to live. They didn't know the way to the way of life. Now, what I'm talking about here tonight is the way to the way of life. What people have done is to steal life and try to build forms according to their concepts of how things should be. With our human minds we don't know how things should be. Our human mind is a very, very limited organ – and it is just an organ, just like my heart, or my stomach, or my liver. My mind is an organ, and we have been run by our organs. Life created the mind; life knows how to use the mind. This plant here couldn't say, 'I want to be a daffodil.' It didn't have any rights; it is just allowed that which it is to be. But man has a right to choose. We can experience life in a much more intense form than this lower aspect of creation can. So man's mind has been stealing life. That's a pretty good commandment, 'Thou shalt not steal.' Most people think of it as taking money from the till. But that's not stealing; that's robbery. True stealing is when we take life. This is the theft, when we take life and try to build a form with our brilliant minds. We try to build a form, as if life didn'a have a design and life didn't know how to build a form. Look at it! Life put me together in 280 days, nine months – imagine that! Isn't that a miracle? It knew what it was doing. We have to unlearn what was learned. We have to learn how to allow the design which is inherent in life to build its own forms.

Now with our minds we don't know what they should be. But who wants to know anyway? Human beings, in the state of thievery in which they exist, always want a preview of coming attractions: 'How's it going to work out?' They want to know that so that what they thought of as intelligence will see if it is good. How is it going to work out? Who cares how it is going to work out? If you are letting life live you, you know it is going to work out fine. What about you? It worked out fine, didn't it? You mean to say you were put together without a Ph.D.? Life creates, and life creates its own forms. You know, there is a very excellent statement in in the Bible: 'Except the Lord build the house, they labour in vain that build it.' Now this word *Lord*. Who is the Lord? Some father figure up in the sky? The Lord is life. Let's paraphrase that: Except life build the house, they labor in vain that build it. Life built this house, didn't it? This is my house. I move and have my being in my house. Most people are paying too much rent on the house – that's why they are overweight. Who built this house? 'Oh,' you say, 'life built it.' All right, well there is another word –

Lord; life. Except life build the house, they labor in vain that build it.

I told you about my relatives, didn't I? Every one of them proved the fact of laboring in vain, every last one of them. Why? Because they tried to build their own house; they didn't let life build the house. If life isn't building your house you're going to labor in vain. In order not to labor in vain we need to begin to be concerned with life. Most human beings say they love life and yet they do everything to forfeit it, they do everything to throw it away. Because if a person is dying it isn't life that is leaving him; it is the person that is leaving life. Life doesn't leave us; we have been leaving life. You never heard of dead life, did you? Life doesn't die. And yet human beings have the experience of dying, don't they? Is that life's design? Do you think life is the author of death? That would be a contradiction, wouldn't it? They're at different poles. We even have death on earth. Now here is a touchy subject. Human beings even think they're liable to die. They are sure of that, aren't they? They think it is normal to die, even though they do everything to prevent it. It is a completely abnormal situation. It isn't life's design that we have this; life isn't the author of death. It exists because man has been moving away from life. And the longer a person is on earth the less and less life they have. They say, 'Oh, when I was a kid I had all kinds of life, but now I need Geritol.' The longer we live, if we are letting life live us, the more life we should have. Why? Because we have more capacity to express it. It should be an increased experience. But human beings in their present state of consciousness, the older they get, what happens? It's like a little clock running down, isn't it? They shrivel up. That isn't life's design. If we say that is life's design, well there is no hope then, is there? At least I'm offering a challenge. At least I'm not saying everything is going to remain the same. At least I'm saying that there is a different way. It is nonsense what we see happening on earth. But it doesn't need to happen; life is not the author of death. Human beings have been dying because they are concerned with the form and not with life. Look at this. There are two things here, right? There is a form and there is life, right? Two things. Where is your identity? Is your identity with the form or is it with that which runs the form? Who are you?

I was up in Canada recently at McMaster University, and they introduced me as an American. When I got up I said, 'I'm not an American,' and all the Canadians smiled. Then I said, 'Thank God I'm not a Canadian!' Life isn't any of these things. Life isn't a Turk or a Greek or a Catholic or a Presbyterian or a Jew. My, wouldn't that be horrible? Made in the image and likeness of a Turk! Life isn't any of these things. You are not any of these things. But if your identity is with the form rather than with life, when you identify yourself you will have all kinds of names after your identity. You will say, 'I'm an American,' or 'I'm a Presbyterian,' or 'I'm a Methodist,' or 'I'm a Catholic.' You see that? 'I am' is life. This is what 'I am' is. Who do you think is talking to you now? A Presbyterian? No. Life is talking to you. When you say 'I am,' who do you think says 'I am'? Did you ever hear a corpse say it? Why don't corpses say 'I am'? No life! So if you say 'I am,' who says it? Life! It is who you are, you are life. And when you are who you are – life – you build the right forms. You build something beautiful – you build a beautiful environment, you build a paradise. People want a paradise, they want a utopia. If we're going to have utopia we've got to be utopian people, haven't we? Can you imagine a slob that is unhappy and sad and complaining and bitching, and he says, 'Well I'd like to get in that paradise.' It wouldn't stay paradise very long if he got in there. No. When you trace your identity back, you are life. But our identity has been with the form, our identity has been with the capacity through which life expresses.

If a person is sick, physically sick, what do they say? 'I'm sick,' right? The body is sick and he says, 'I'm sick.' Or the mind is confused and he says, 'I'm confused.' No, you're not confused. It is your mind that is confused. Or if you are emotionally upset and you say, 'I'm disturbed.' 'I am' is never disturbed, by the way. Did you ever hear of disturbed life? You might rightly say, 'My body is sick, my mind is confused, my emotions are disturbed, but I am fine.' Do you know why the body is sick? Do you know why the mind is confused? Do you know why the emotions are disturbed? Just because we haven't been who we are. Do you think life makes the body sick? Life creates it; it doesn't make it sick. The reason it gets sick is because we are not expressing what we are – life. Do you think life confuses the mind? Life created the mind. When life is using the mind we have brilliant thoughts, we have life's thoughts. They are original thoughts; they are not canned. And when life is using the capacity of emotion which it created we have some delightful feelings. And all this experience has nothing to do with the environment, nothing at all. Our identity has been with the form, with the flesh, and not with life.

When a person begins to see this, when he begins to see that he has been using life in darkened understanding, he begins to pay attention to the thing that he needs to pay attention to. Do you know what we need to pay attention to? We need to pay attention to life. A person says, 'Well, that's good. How do you do that?' Well life has a certain character, life has a certain quality. First of all, life is happy. That is one of life's characteristics. If you are expressing the character of life, the true character of you, you are happy. It has nothing to do with environment; it has nothing to do with who is around you or who isn't around you. It has nothing to do with the job you are doing or the job you are not doing. That has nothing to do with it. Life is happy! That is life's character, and if you are expressing life you are happy.

Now most people, when they consider happiness, what do they think about? You'll notice it is always projected to the future, isn't it? 'When I get to a certain point then I'll be happy.' That's nonsense! You know why? They are thinking they are unhappy now because they are not living, because they are not expressing life, because they are phonies. They may say, 'I'm unhappy now because of this environment. When I get out of this environment and I get into another environment, boy, watch me shine!' Oh no. You are going to bring that same consciousness of self into that other environment. You know what you are going to be? The same way – unhappy. It has nothing to do with environment. Life is happy. So when you pay attention to life you express the quality of happiness. You don't look around with your brilliant mind and say, 'Now wait, should I be happy? Things should be just the way I like them.' No, you don't even look around. If people were to look at your environment they would say, 'What the hell is that guy happy for?' That's your so-called friends, by the way. They are telling you about the things that are wrong. No, you just express happiness because that is life's nature. And, you know, you will find that when you express life, happiness, your environment will begin to reflect it. You will find that the forms that life is building will begin to appear in your environment. That is the way it will work out. You see, we've got everything backward. It is life that is supposed to build the form, not our brilliant mind. The identity of you. Who was the French philosopher? Descartes. He said, 'I think, therefore I am.' Baloney! 'I am, therefore I think.' He got de cart before de horse. There is something that precedes thinking; there is something that created the mind. Life! And your identity is with life, is with cause. The mind is only an effect. The mind is the result of life. You are not the result of life; you are life. And when you are identified with life you may say, 'I am, therefore I think, and I think correctly. I think thoughts that are life's thoughts.'

I saw a little cartoon in the paper the other day. A little insipid professor, he said, 'I think, therefore I am, I think.' There is always doubt. When your identity is with your equipment, of which the mind is part, rather than with life, you will always feel insecure, full of fear. But when we are identified with life we know that all things do work together to perfection for those who maintain their life connection. Things work out fine. And you know the most interesting part about it? With your mind you don't know how they are going to work out. That's the adventure! What's going to work out here? It isn't anything that is laid out before you; it is something that works out. Did you ever spell love backward? Evol. It is something that evolves. And this is a natural, evolving process.

Now I've seen many human beings who have begun to catch the vision and stopped trying to live life and let life live them. Consequently they have been expressing the characteristics of life, the qualities of life, and things have begun to change in their environment. But then they shifted. They said, 'Oh, wait a minute. That shouldn't be and that should be and that . . . ,' and they were right back, identified with the form again. With our mind we don't know what should be, we haven't got the slightest clue, and if you are letting life live you you don't care. 'Oh you should plan,' they say, 'you should have goals.' All my relatives did, they had goals and plans, but they are all failures. I'm not going to travel that route. I'm concerned with success. I'm concerned with creation – with integration, not disintegration. When I speak of integration, look at man; he wants integration. Of all the stupid things, he goes and passes a law which is a lot of nonsense; they put it on the books that you have to integrate. You see this form, this physical body? Integration, right? It was the undifferentiated earth at one time and here it is integrated. What integrated this? What brought it together? Life did, didn't it? Can you imagine human beings, not expressing the characteristics of life, trying to get together? It's impossible. There should be integration, of course. We are all one, life is one. We're not Canadians and Presbyterians and Americans and Greeks and Italians. We are life. When we express what we are we find ourselves integrated; not because we tried to crank it out with our human mind, but because life's character is to integrate we begin to come together, we begin to find oneness. And this works out naturally. Life does it!

You know, we have a ranch in Loveland, Colorado, called Sunrise Ranch. I live there six months of the year. And we have people there from everywhere – the strangest conglomeration of people that you can imagine. And, you know something, they are getting along! They are having a ball there. Do you know why? Because, first of all, life brought them together. Believe me, if you saw this conglomerate you'd know only life could do it. It isn't something you can figure out with your mind. But those people there are concerned with one thing: they are concerned with letting life have its way. By the way, life is going to have its way anyway. We need to get with it.

Krishna mentioned, in the *Gita*, that life, 'mighty of appetite, powerful, and strong,' was man's enemy or man's friend. Man has the experience of life being an enemy when he is not with life.

When you are not with life you have the experience of life being an enemy; when you are with life you have the experience of life being a friend. Now, that's life, and contained within it is the design and control. Life created this form called man, male and female, so that it might have a vehicle through which to express its design at this level of creation. And by the way, when it isn't hindered at this level, you notice the beauty; there is beauty in this aspect of creation when it doesn't interfere with life's design. It comes through and we say, 'How beautiful!' Of course; what you are looking at is the truth of life's design.

Now here we have man, created by life, with a capacity for life to use. But man has a mind. Life created man to have a mind so that he could have a greater experience than the lilies of the field. But man's mind has been taking life and saying, 'I'm not going to take that. I'm going to build my own life out here, see.' And here it is. This is what it looks like – a maze. We need to let the mind come to rest. 'Be still and know that I am,' says life, and it says that to our mind. 'Be still. Stop trying to run this show. You are just an effect, not the cause. I am the cause.' And when the mind is still and it isn't cranking, trying to turn things out to its own advantages, according to its concepts of good and evil – when the mind is still, then life begins to use these capacities, and because it uses these capacities and expresses through them there begins to be something beautiful out here. What do we see in our world? Pollution. We see all this distortion in our world. What is it? It is just a reflection of what is in man, that's all; and here he is trying to fix up the pollution when he himself is a mess. To get rid of pollution we have to get rid of him! Pollution is just the effect. Man is the cause of the whole thing because he has been trying to take life and use it. When we come to a state of rest then life begins to express through us. Our particular responsibility is to let life have its way, because the most important thing is life; yet human beings put everything ahead of that, don't they? – their education, their marriage, their relationships, their loot, all this. Everything is put in front of life.

Our sense of values has been so distorted, so warped, so perverted. Life is the thing! And you say, 'Well if I put my values in life, what do I do?' First of all you express happiness, you express kindness, you express joy, you express forgiveness. If you have a character around you who is using life in darkened understanding he is going to trample over you every now and then, and if you resent that guy . . . life doesn't resent; that isn't life's character. If you are identified with life you forgive him, just like that. You don't wait a long time: 'I'd better forgive him.' No. If you are identified with life there is instantaneous forgiveness – everything is instant today – instantaneous forgiveness. Do you know why? Because if you do not forgive him, meaning if you do not express the characteristics of life, you are standing in life's way. Here you are resenting. Do you know what life does to those who resent? Smack! – because we were created to express life and if you are resenting, it can't express; that isn't life's character. You have closed the door on life and you are saying, 'Life's an enemy!' Of course it may seem like an enemy, but it isn't life that is the enemy; it is you who are going contradictory to life, that's all. Change your attitude. The moment you change your attitude life begins to express through you; you are fine, and life is a friend then. But if you hold characteristics, attitudes, that are not true to life's character you are going to be an enemy to life and you will be unhappy and frustrated and depressed. And then you go to some psychiatrist and this psychiatrist says – I don't say these things facetiously, but these things happen – 'Now first of all do you have some money? Yes? Okay. Then you can sit down.' (Life doesn't charge, by the way.) Then he analyzes your childhood. 'You need a new wife . . . you need a new job . . . you need to go to Florida, especially this time of the year.' He gives a guy excuses for being an enemy of life. You know how I counsel when they come to me unhappy? I say, 'Oh, you're self-centered, are you?' Isn't that the truth? Anyone who is unhappy won't say they are self-centered, but anyone who is self-centered is unhappy. Anyone who is unhappy is self-centered. That's all! If you are unhappy, if you are not leading a vibrant, vigorous life, it isn't life's fault; it is your fault, because you are not expressing it, because you are so busy trying to build your little bailiwick. How did your elders make out?

I'm just going to close with a little bit from the *Gita*. What a beautiful book! To human beings, when they take life and try to build their own little forms, they build them according to their concepts, their mental concepts, of what is good or what is bad. 'Never build the bad things. Always build the good things,' and what they think is good turns out to be bad. Did you ever notice that? But they are always trying to build according to their mental concept of good and bad, according to their likes and dislikes. Now get this. This book is literally thousands of years old. Let me read you what they are saying. This is Krishna again. He says this: 'By passion for the "pairs of opposites." ' That's right. People have a passion for this pair of opposites; good and bad, likes and dislikes.

> By passion for the 'pairs of opposites,'
> By those twain snares of Like and Dislike, Prince!
> All creatures live bewildered, save some few
> Who, quit of sins, holy in act, informed,
> Freed from the 'opposites,' and fixed in faith,
> Cleave unto Me.

That's it! Those twin snares – trying to build things according to likes and dislikes, good and evil, and you end up in the box, like my relatives. How wonderful it is, what a tremendous privilege it is, to have the facilities life created here on earth, to have a body and a mind, and this beautiful capacity of emotional release; for it is through this capacity that we can express the quality and characteristics of life. And when we begin to do it, do you know what happens? We begin to be an influence on others. By the way, the word *influence* means 'in the flow.' If we are in the flow of life, if we are letting life have its way with us – not trying to steal life and build according to our concepts of good and evil but letting life have its way – we begin to be an influence on others. Not because we preach, not because we tell them what sinners they are, but because in our living we are an inspiration to others. They see the joy and the love and the assurance and the wholesomeness that is finding expression through our capacities and they say, 'My I'd like your experience.' And those who are doing it, those who are letting life live them, just say, 'Follow me. Let that which is true of me be true of you. Let life have its way with you. Let life build that which it would build.' And as you do, you begin to realize that this is just a wonderful planet to be living on at this time.

It is wonderful to be here. It is wonderful to be in expression that which we are in reality.

A talk given at the University of Colorado in Boulder, Colorado, March 25, 1971.

PAY ATTENTION TO LIFE

William Bahan

What is it that really counts? What is it that is the thing of true value?

Some years ago, in New York City, I was giving a series of lectures and also doing some counseling, and I had a couple come to me in pretty tough shape emotionally. After I had seen them a few times they came in one day and they were really high – oh my, they were all excited! They hadn't been that way before; they were really a couple of glum plums.

'What's all the excitement about?' I asked.

And they said, 'Our name has been picked to be one of the probable winners in the New York State Sweepstakes – $1,000,000.'

'Well, I suppose $1,000,000 has its value,' I said, 'but I know something that's actually more valuable.'

'Oh, what's that?' they say.

'Life.'

They laugh. 'Oh, Bill, you're always saying things like that.'

'Okay, let's say your name is picked on that sweepstakes and the State of New York gives me the million dollars to take to you, but before I can get the money to you, you die. There you are, laid out in a box, and I come in with a million dollars. I lay it down beside you and I say, "Live it up! Have a good time!"'

Money isn't really that valuable, is it? Life is the thing that's valuable, but strangely enough we seem to do everything to throw it away. People squander it. Talk about spendthrifts! We throw it away, but when we begin to run out of it we really start to clamor – 'Help me, help me!' But for those who begin to recognize true values, they realize that the supreme value is life. If one has found that, he has found the pearl of great price. Now when I say this a person sometimes replies, 'Well I think that's nice, but how do you put your values in life?' You see, in our experience of what we call living our values have been external; everything has been out here; the million-dollar New York Sweepstakes seem so important. We forget about the fact that there is an invisible aspect to our being called life. You've never seen life. Have you ever noticed that? You see the evidence of the presence of life, but you've never seen life. And because we can't see it we tend to say, 'Well, what's really of value is the finger.' We can't see the thing that's moving the finger, so that must not be too important; but the finger, that's really important! And so we get all wrapped up in the finger – the material aspect. But if we ignore the invisible aspect and just pay attention to the visible, we're only considering half of us.

I heard a story recently about a very famous judge in New York who was known for being able to hand down more decisions than any other judge in the United States. The reporters asked him how he was able to do this.

'Well,' the judge said, 'the plaintiff comes, I listen to her, and then I hand down a decision.'

A reporter asked, 'But how about the defense? Don't you listen to them?'

'I used to,' said the judge, 'but it just confused me.'

So there are always two aspects, and if both aren't considered you have imbalance. We have a world that is unbalanced, and it's unbalanced because we ignore this other vital aspect of our being, life! We become all centered in the external, the visible, and we ignore the invisible. Yet true value lies, actually, in the invisible, and because we do ignore the invisible we have imbalances. First of all, any physical disease is but an imbalance; that's all it is. All diseases are either too much or too little. You either have diarrhea or you're constipated. If your thyroid gland is working too much you have hyperthyroidism. If your thyroid gland isn't putting out enough thyroxine you have hypothyroidism. Medical science has these two words – *hyper* and *hypo*. Hyper, too much; hypo, too little. Hypertension, high blood pressure; hypotension, low blood pressure. And then human beings, ignoring the invisible aspect of their being, think to set a balance in the visible. So what do they try to do to set the balance? They hypo the hyper and they hyper the hypo.

Do you know one of the greatest problems in the North American continent today? We cannot build enough mental hospitals fast enough. If someone's having problems mentally they say he's mentally unbalanced. Now, how are we going to set the balance in that? Are we going to restore mental balance by adjusting external situations? No, we must assist this person to begin to recognize that the physical and the mental can be in balance only because there's something back of these capacities that's always in balance. All of our attention has been up front. Even with our cigarette ads we say, 'It's what's up front that counts.' But it isn't; it's what's behind.

In our world situation we are at a point where we could topple because of this imbalance. Human beings are always trying to achieve a balance of power between nations. It never works, for it all comes back to the individual, it all comes back to you and me. Where is our center of orientation? Where do we place our sense of values? In considering this let us draw a circle on the blackboard to represent a creative field. In a creative field there are various levels of what we might call vibrations. Did you ever wonder, for instance, why we have roses and pansies and daisies – the

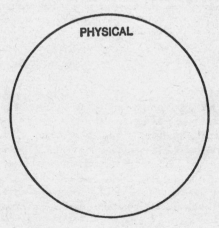

ones that don't tell? We have these different kinds of flowers because each has a different level of vibration but all of them on the observable, physical level.

So out here on the periphery of our creative field we have what we could rightly call the physical – our physical bodies, for instance. This arm seems to really be the solid, you know. I can touch it. That's hard, solid, or at least so it appears.

Now, we have the physical because of a particular level of vibration. The physical includes many things – minerals, flowers, animals. This is all the periphery of a creative field. Isn't it interesting that man identifies himself with the periphery of this creative field? He identifies himself as an animal, doesn't he? He apparently thinks of himself as the king of the beasts. When you identify yourself as an animal you're out there on the periphery. There's nothing wrong with the animal being out there, but we shouldn't be.

As I've mentioned, in this creative field there are various levels of vibration, and the level of vibration determines the nature of the form. There is another level of form in our experience. It's called the mental. We have a mind, and it's on a different level of vibration than the physical level – we might say a more refined level.

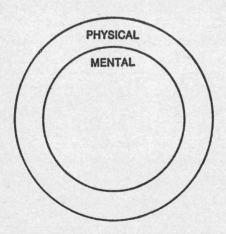

We need balance in all of these levels. If a person is sick, as I mentioned, it's because of an imbalance. If a person isn't balanced mentally, well he needs help. How do you think this help is going to come? Is it going to come by working out here, hypo and hypering? Is it going to come because some learned man listens to our mind regurgitate its problems and says, 'Oh yes, what you need is to go to Florida'? I was just there. Believe me, there are lots of problems down there. No, balance can't be set mentally or physically, because there are other levels which determine these external levels.

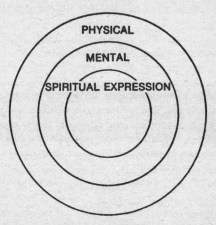

Now, there's a level of vibration which is more refined than the mind. It is a level which most people completely ignore; they know nothing about it because it's higher than the mind. It's called the level of spiritual expression. And, you know, being at a higher vibratory level, the mind cannot penetrate into it. We may be most thankful it can't. There are those who go through all kinds of mental gymnastics trying to penetrate with their mind into this higher level of vibration, but they can't.

So, here are various levels of vibration, but that leaves *you* unaccounted for. Where are you? Who are you? Who are you anyway? If our identity is out there we don't know who we are.

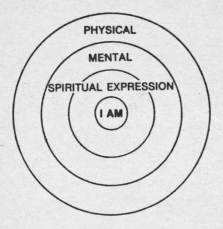

Actually we are right in here, in the core – 'I am.' And those are words that bring us to focus. You say 'I.' Who's speaking? Who is speaking when you say 'I'? If our identity is out there then we're identified with the wrong *I*. The *I* that is what we are is right here. Because our values haven't been right here, but rather out there, we're not too happy. Oh, we have flashes probably when we're happy because everything's right for the moment. Did you ever notice, though, you never seem to get things to stay right? Whenever you get both ends together someone always seems to move the other end? 'I was happy yesterday, but I'm not too happy today.' Happiness is determined by circumstances when identity is with the peripheral level. And if your happiness is dependent upon your circumstances you have a yo-yo experience. 'Everything's going right. Oh boy!' But then, 'Not too good today.' And you're up and you're down, you're up and you're down.

People say, 'Well that's life, you know.' No, it isn't! No, it isn't! That may be the experience that you call life, but it isn't life. Life is here, represented by the center of this diagram. You are that which is moving the finger. You are life. This is who you are. You *are.* When you say, 'I am,' who's that that's speaking? It's life that's speaking and life is happy. It's strong. It's capable. But our identity hasn't been at that core. And because it hasn't been at that core, because we haven't expressed the truth of ourselves from here, there have been all kinds of imbalances out there on the periphery.

I was reading recently that scientists have recognized what they call a fourth state of matter. We knew from our high school physics that there are three states of matter: there is the solid, the periphery; there is the liquid, which would actually come to focus in the mind – water, something fluid; there is the air, and in most people their spiritual realm is rather nebulous. The fourth state they call plasma – that would be right here in the center of our diagram. And do you know what they said that fourth state of matter is made of? The same stuff that stars are made of. And you know what stars are. Every star is a sun. So that fourth dimension, that fourth level, would be sun substance. And what force is symbolical of the sun? Fire. Now, most people don't have much fire, do they? But do you know that when a person begins to find out who he is, when he knows that reality of the plasma as being himself, he knows fire? You're the fire. How do you feel? If you're not identified with the fire, you may feel burnt-out. But you, in fact, are the fire. In order to come to experience that fire, we need to begin to take our identity away from this periphery, and the only way that we can do that is to recognize that there is something more important. If we're all centered in the imbalance, trying to set the imbalance right, well we'll never leave there. Most people say, 'I'd like to pay attention to this, the source of the fire, but look at this thing over here! I've got to straighten that out first.'

I often think of the Shepherd's Psalm, which says, 'Thou preparest a table before me in the presence of mine enemies.' Now, most people never come to the table. They're too busy with their enemies. They want to get rid of their enemies first. But do you know something? Enemies are going to stay around. Sickness, that's an enemy, isn't it? Fight heart trouble! Fight cancer! Mother's march on tired blood! I'm not saying these things facetiously; I'm just saying we've got everything backwards. We're trying to set a balance out in the periphery and it's impossible to do it there.

As we look at our world we find that most people have these four levels of themselves unbalanced. For instance, this level of spiritual expression, which we might say is the third dimensional level, with most people is absolutely immature, absolutely. The physical and mental levels are highly developed: we have all kinds of colleges of physical education and yoga; we have all kinds of universities and colleges for intellectual development. But let me ask you: How many of us actually received any training for the development of spiritual expression? If emphasis is put on the development of only these two outer levels – and it certainly has been – then we'll find that we're top-heavy. Did you ever see a disturbed Ph.D.? He's very heavy up here in the head, lots of expansion, but emotionally he's a dwarf, emotionally he's completely immature. And if we are immature in these inner levels there will definitely be imbalance on the physical and mental planes. But if we begin to accept new values and realize that these invisible realms within ourselves are the things of first importance, and if we put them first in our living, then certain things begin to happen in what we call consciousness.

In religious circles – and that's a very apt description, by the way, circles – they speak of the fall of man. No one ever tells you what fell, have you noticed that? Man's arches, or what? What was it that fell? It was his consciousness. Man in a true state of consciousness should be at center, expressing the 'I am' identity. But unfortunately our identity has been out in these peripheral realms. Consequently our consciousness needs to rise up to the level where we rightly belong. But in order for the consciousness of people to lift up they must have their values straight; they must recognize that true values are in these finer realms of being, and they must pay attention to them.

As a person begins to do something in fact about the quality and nature of his spiritual expression, changes begin to work out in his consciousness. It was Thoreau, I believe, who remarked that man fell but no one ever thinks of getting up. Well how about getting up! People say, 'Oh well, we're sinners. We're sinners.' A sinner is someone who is identified out here in the periphery. I don't know if you know anything about archery, but if you don't hit the bull's-eye and your arrow misses the target, do you know what they call that? A sin. In archery, that's called a sin. And that's all sin is. We're just not hitting the bull's-eye; we're out here, away from the mark.

I recently came across a very interesting book called *Fields Within Fields*. There's an article here by a psychologist from a university in Virginia. I'd like to read some of the tremendous things that he's recognizing. Listen to this:

'It now seems highly plausible that the seat of consciousness will never be found by a neurosurgeon, because it appears to involve not so much an organ or organs, but the interaction of energy fields within the brain. These patterns of energy would be disrupted by surgical intervention and have long since disappeared in cadavers. Neurophysiologists will not likely find what they are looking for outside their own consciousness, for that which they are looking for is that which is looking.' (*Fields Within Fields,* Winter 1973–74, 'Of Time and the Mind,' by Keith Floyd, p. 56.)

Absolutely! Anyone who has in fact offered truly creative self-expression on earth has come to the point where he recognized that he was the thing that was looking. Such people begin to find their identity centered in this realm here, in this core, in this fourth dimension, which is beyond the realm of space and time. The consciousness of human beings has been in a three-dimensional coffin, dying. We didn't come on earth to have an experience of living in a three-dimensional coffin; we came on earth to express the truth of life. It isn't something separate from you or me. And for those who have expressed this truth, something has happened in their consciousness. Their pattern of association has changed, so that they came to the point where they recognized 'I am that.' Moses, you remember, came to the point where he recognized, 'I am that I am.' He realized that he was the thing that was looking. 'I am that I am.'

In relationship to Moses, do you recall that he was a murderer? He murdered a man in Egypt. He lost his temper – emotionally immature – and he murdered a man and he had to hotfoot it out of Egypt. It seemed like a tragic experience, but it was in fact the turning point in his particular experience on earth. That was a great thing that happened to him. Do you know why? Because in Egypt he was all wrapped up in these outer planes. Then an incident happened which revealed his imbalance; he murdered a man. He had to hotfoot it out of Egypt, and he had no more distraction. He found himself on the backside of the desert and he had to allow a change of values to come. He began to pay attention to certain qualities within himself that he had been completely unaware of.

Do you know why we have been unaware of our true selves? Because we've had a great big hole in our heart – here in the connecting link between our mind and the reality which we are. But when we begin to pay attention, as Moses did, to things of true value, we come to the point where our pattern of association is right. We aren't a 'sinner' anymore. We aren't out on the periphery. And you know, as you read the story, Moses didn't want to accept this, he didn't want to accept the truth of himself. Very few people do. They prefer to say, 'I'm a sinner.' All right, we know that, we can see that. Let's stop stating the obvious. We've all played that game. But how few there are who will accept the great challenge and begin to accept the truth of themselves. At first Moses wanted it to be done by the hand of somebody else; but it couldn't be done by the hand of somebody else, because nobody else saw it. And if you see it, if you have the vision, then *you* have the responsibility. There's no one else at the center of your being but you.

We have the responsibility to express the nature and the quality of that center point. And as we do, then what do you think would happen in these outer realms of experience? Do you think our bodies would be sick and falling apart? Do you think we'd be building more mental hospitals? Do you think we'd have this state of emotional immaturity? No. There would be balance. Our bodies would reveal the beauty of the form which life would build. And our minds would begin to share the most beautiful thought patterns one could imagine. Most people can't stand their thoughts. Did you ever hear a person say, 'I hate to think about it'? They can't stand their own thought pattern. And what would we be feeling in this capacity for spiritual expression? Do you think it would be full of fear, as it is with most people, or full of resentment, or full of jealousy, or full of anger and full of doubt? Oh, no. We would experience the greatest intensity of love in this capacity. But it's all consequent upon our coming to this point of centering. And we don't have to commit murder to begin to pay attention to it. We don't have to get into a jam before we pay attention to it. Most people have to be knocked down before they look up.

But coming back to what I particularly want to emphasize this evening, you can't come to this point of centering in consciousness without first giving attention to what I've termed the level of spiritual expression. You can't come to it with your mind, believe me. You can't study to get to it. You come to it when you begin to pay attention to the spiritual expression level. In this connection it is interesting to read the record of what's in the Bible. Do you know what these two Testaments are? They're a record of man's failure – not all men; I mentioned Moses, and of course there was that great one, Jesus – but generally, it is a record of man's failure. The Bible records the opportunities that were offered to man to begin to get up, lift up, rise up, and come back to where he should be in conscious identity. The Old Testament is a record of the physical approach; it was a physical approach because that's where man's consciousness was, and you need to work with people where they are. If you have a five-year-old child, you don't start in with geometry lessons. You need to pick him up where he is and begin to teach him one and one are two and two and two are four. And man was down at that stage, and what was offered to him was something at that level. And as you read the story you see that it was rejected. It worked out for quite a while, but finally, at the time of Solomon, it went kaput! Then another level was offered. The New Testament records the ministry of Jesus and what He offered on the mental level, what today we translate as 'belief.' He was serving at this level because that's where man was at the time; that's why He was found in the temple with the scholars. But this approach was rejected, flatly rejected, along with the one who brought it.

And now you and I are here today. Those two approaches –

physical and mental – have gone by the board; they're all gone. We can't make the collective physical approach any more; it's gone. We can't make a mental approach in trying to come to our reality; that opportunity is gone too. Those approaches were right and timely when they were offered, but now there's something new needed. The approach which man *must* make today, absolutely *must*, is the approach through the capacity of spiritual expression. If we're going to come into the fourth dimension we have to come in through the third. Our world right now is like a ballplayer who's up at the plate and he has two strikes on him – he's missed the first one, and he's missed the second one. And you know what happens when you miss the third one – you're out! Man has the tools today by which to count himself out. He can't destroy the earth but he can do a very effective job of destroying the forms of life on earth. He can't destroy life but he can destroy the forms of life, and our physical bodies happen to be one of the forms.

You and I are here on earth. You and I have a very vital part to play in offering that balanced state into our world. It doesn't matter what occupation we have in the world, as long as it's honorable; it has nothing to do with worldly position. What it has to do with is the nature and the quality of what we express. If that which we express is true to the truth of what we are then we are offering a creative influence into our world, and it is that creative influence which can change the world, bring it to a state of balance.

A talk given in Loveland, Colorado, April 23, 1974, as subsequently edited for *The Emissary* magazine.

THE CYCLES OF MATURITY

William Bahan

I've entitled our consideration 'The Cycles of Maturity.' If there are any here who think that they are completely mature, they may leave before we start. I'm sure if we have a degree of modesty we have no takers in relationship to that. The most wonderful part about experiencing maturity is the fact that it is something that already is. Human beings in fact are mature. Unfortunately they have been identified with that which is immature. Now, in order to experience this maturity which we are going to consider this evening we need to initially recognize that we are in a very, very sad state of immaturity. Actually the greatest need in the world today is for men and women who are mature.

I was recently handed a cartoon. Paradoxically it shows a lecture hall, and up on the board it says: 'Today's lecture, "Man, Master of the Universe," has been canceled because of the natural gas shortage.' Perhaps we could take that word *man* out, as the master of the universe – he doesn't even know the cause of the common cold – and probably we could insert the name *God*, the master of the universe. But if this reality which we call God is to reveal the fact of mastery on earth it must have some vehicle; this reality called God must have some vehicle through which it can reveal its mastery. And man, that homo sapiens, the one who calls himself the crowning creation, has in fact been created for the purpose of being the means by which the reality of God may have mastery on earth. Now, as long as man is concerned with his own little thing, this mastery which is a fact already isn't experienced. The reality of man is mature, but he hasn't been identified with that which is mature. I was recently reading a little ditty in a *Wildlife* magazine; I think I wrote it down:

Strange that man should make up lists
Of living things in danger.
Why he fails to list himself
Is really even stranger.

He is in fact in danger, very much so. If anyone has any sort of vision and lifts his eyes high enough to see what's moving in the world it could engender tremendous fear. Now if this danger is to be rectified it certainly isn't going to be rectified by man in his present state of consciousness. It's going to be rectified when we have mature men and women on earth by which this reality called God may reveal its mastery. So I thought we might consider the cycles of maturity and outline how it may work out that you and I may be a revelation of mature men and women on earth.

We'll start where we should start – in the beginning. And in the beginning, do you know that you and I from the outer standpoint were just one little cell? The sperm of our father and the ovum of our mother came together, and in 280 lunar days that reality, called life or God, took those two germs and built a living form. So we started with one cell and the cycle worked out; the babe was born. And at that particular point in our physical development we did have a state of consciousness. We had a baby state of consciousness.

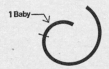

Now I don't think we can remember it too well, but it was our initial state of consciousness, the consciousness of the babe. This reality didn't leave us just as a baby. It kept moving and it kept developing this form, and we passed out of the baby stage and came to the physical development of the child. With that child form we had a child state of consciousness.

Now you will note that as we're moving along in this developing form it is changing and consequently the consciousness continues

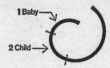

to change. But at these particular stages in development the consciousness that we had was consequent upon the form: baby form, baby consciousness; child form, child consciousness. So we finished that child cycle, at least physically, and life continued on, continued developing the form; and the form moved on out of the child state and we came into the age of adolescence. And we had a particular state of consciousness that was consequent upon that physical development; we had an adolescent state of consciousness.

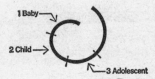

Now you can see, as I am emphasizing, that our consciousness is consequent upon the developing form. The consciousness emerges out of the form at that particular state; there's nothing wrong with it. That's the way it should be. By the way, in these changing states of physical development and in the development of the consciousness there is a continuing self-centeredness because our centering is in the form. Being centered in the form we are naturally self-centered. There is nothing wrong with that either. As long as a person's consciousness arises out of the form, he is self-centered. I've often seen mothers trying to make little children selfless. Of all the nonsense! If your child is self-centered he's perfectly normal.

So here are three aspects, three phases, of the physical development. Then we move into the development of the adult physical body, and we have an adult consciousness. Now you'll notice that I didn't call that a matured state of consciousness. We have an

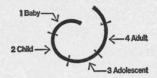

adult consciousness consequent upon the fact that we have an adult body. Now, unfortunately, most human beings get off the train at this point – they stop. There are some changes in this adult state of consciousness: there's the young adult, the middle-aged adult, and the old adult. But the state of consciousness at that point, with most people, stops emerging or unfolding. What should happen of course is that the cycle should go on; the consciousness should begin to emerge out of the physical body. Unfortunately, because of a lack of understanding, and also in many people a total unwillingness to allow further changes to take place, we move in a circle rather than a cycle. And you'll note as people get older, what happens to them? They call it second childhood! This is usually considered the way. As people get older they get childish, and they say, 'Oh, we're getting old,' as if that's the natural state! But you can see how this cycle ends up. It stops being a cycle and ends up as a circle – the ultimate nothing, a great big cipher. Human

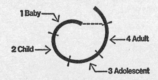

beings, usually toward what they call the end of their life span on earth, the December of their living, feel that way – nothing. Even those who were considered great leaders in the world, or the intellectuals of the world, have this experience. I read one time that Einstein, when he came to the December of his life, was reported to have said, 'If only I had known, I should have become a watchmaker.' Winston Churchill said, 'I'm bored.' Now this shouldn't be the experience. We need to move on through from the baby stage to the adult stage and continue beyond these four.

We have four different phases, four different cycles, very specific cycles. Now this has been portrayed many times through symbolic writings. For instance, in the Bible we see 40 mentioned frequently. You'll remember that at the time of Noah it rained for 40 days and 40 nights. The Children of Israel wandered in the wilderness for 40 years. And in the experience of Jesus, He was in the wilderness 40 days. Why not 38 or 22, or something like that? Why 40? Because there were very definite cycles working out. You might say that this particular pattern of the physical development and the changing states of consciousness could be actually defined as the wilderness. And man, moving through this wilderness, has had a tough time seemingly, because he hasn't been moving perfectly with it. He has in fact stopped, and his consciousness of himself continues to arise out of his physical body. He does not know who he is, and it's a tough proposition. When he stopped, he stopped under a ceiling. And of course if we have stopped under a

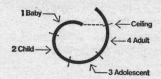

ceiling, we're constantly bumping our heads on that ceiling; we feel restricted, we feel inhibited. There are those under the ceiling who say, 'Well this is just the proving ground, here on earth. The big show is on the other side.' I don't see anyone hurrying to get to the other side. No, the big show is right here. It seems like a little show because we are so restricted. And, as I say, it's a tough bit under this ceiling. Things seem hard; things seem difficult; we have a cross to bear. I read a little story the other day about that:

When Johnny arrived home from Sunday school his father asked, 'What did you learn in Sunday school this morning?'

'Oh,' said Johnny, 'we learned about a bear named Gladly. He was cross-eyed.'

'You learned about a bear named Gladly that was cross-eyed?'

'Yeah. We even sang a song about him: "Gladly, the cross-eyed bear!"'

Do you ever feel like that, bearing a heavy cross? Yesterday morning on television Governor Brown said, 'Life and human nature never change.' I would agree in relationship to human nature, but that isn't the reality of life. Tonight on the news a Washingtonian said, 'Life is very unjust.' I have no doubt that there are many injustices in the world – there sure are lots of injustice collectors – but life isn't unjust. Could this magnificent reality be unjust which took those two little germs that we were and in 280 days built a baby form? It didn't put our ear on our navel, or anything else like that. It was pretty nice about the whole thing, I think, very intelligent. Yes, there are injustices in human experience, but it has nothing to do with life. All of this difficulty that human beings know, all of the injustices, all of the tough sledding, is all consequent upon the human experience underneath this ceiling. As long as we stay under the ceiling, that's our experience. We experience what's called human nature, and human nature is a nature which derives out of our physical form. We bring forth our ancestral characteristics. You know, it's said those ancestral characteristics were visited upon the third and fourth generation. I've always appreciated that word *visited*. It didn't mean they had to stay! They can leave, you know.

As long as we continue to find ourselves identified with human nature, we're caught underneath this ceiling; and there is no way in human nature that we can penetrate it. Actually it is a ceiling which can be penetrated, but it can't be penetrated as long as we maintain an identity which emerges out of the physical form. The reality brought the form up to this point to use it for its own purposes. If our identity is allowed to emerge through this ceiling, we would find that rather than being with the physical form, our identity would be with the reality which brought up the form. Now there's the thing. When human beings who are under the ceiling say, 'I am,' their identity emerges out of the physical form and they say, 'I am Italian,' or 'I am Jewish,' or 'I am Catholic,' or 'I am Protestant.' Can you imagine this reality being Irish, or

Jewish, or Catholic, or Protestant? That isn't the truth of ourselves. If our identity emerges through the ceiling we say in truth, 'I am life.'

There was One who walked on earth nineteen centuries ago who came through that ceiling, who came through that door. It's an open door, by the way; there's nothing blocking it. He came through the door, and because He came through the door He knew who He was. He said, 'I am the way, the truth and the life. I am love, truth, and life. My identity is with the reality. The Father and I are one.' Here was One on earth who revealed maturity. He grew up, and in a short span, 30 years actually. You might remember that at the age of 12 He had a realization. His mother wanted Him to do certain things; I think she wanted to keep Him hooked into the pattern that she was in. He answered His mother and said, 'Wist ye not that I must be about my Father's business?' At that particular point in His consciousness He recognized that He needed to stay with the reality that was bringing the form up, that which He called the Father. And He did stay with it. He came through that ceiling. He came through that seeming veil, and coming through it He knew who He was – a mature man on earth, I Am. He said, 'I am come that they might have life, and that they might have it more abundantly.' What did you come for? Do you think that you can come to bring life if you're not identified with life? We came on earth for exactly the same reason. Any person who reaches maturity knows that: 'I am come that they might have life.' That's what's missing! This world is a great big morgue, a large graveyard. Life needs to be known, and in order to know life we must be identified with life. And being identified with life, we know who we are. Because we know who we are we know why we're here, we know what we need to do. First of all, we need to express life. We need to be who we are. A person says, 'Be who you are.' Good idea! But we certainly don't know who we are as long as our identity emerges out of the form.

We might begin to recognize why this cycle turns into a circle. As it's coming along the way in the developing stages of the form, human beings lose their alignment with life. There are so many things that take the person off the track, so many distractions.

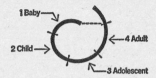

Response by human beings is given to externals more than to the reality which is building the form. We become misaligned as far as life is concerned. I mentioned that One who at the age of 12 recognized that He must be about the Father's business. He realized at that age that He needed to stay in alignment with life, that that was the important thing. It is the important thing. Most of us are over 12 and we have an adult physical body. We have this beautiful facility created by life to be used by life. Now it hasn't been used by life. It's very easy to see if life is using your form; very simple checks may be made. You'll find that those who are under the ceiling, who haven't come on through to the point where they know their true identity centers in life, will always need to be encouraged. Do you need to be encouraged? It is a cardinal symptom of immaturity; you're hitting the ceiling. Those in this state always need to be inspired. Some of them come to my talks sometimes! 'Boy, you really inspire me,' they say. I usually see them a week later – flat tires! They need to be pumped up again, recharged like a battery. Did you ever hear anyone say, 'Oh, that really charges my battery!' What a leech that is! They wouldn't need their battery charged if their generator was working. And the generator is only working in a person's experience when he is identified with life.

Externals keep taking us off the track. All these things in our environment become so important; they seem so big. One of the things that seems so big is our mind. Just because a person becomes intellectually big doesn't mean he is mature, any more than a person who becomes physically big. Actually, the bigger the mind becomes and the more swelled up it becomes in its knowledge of how things should be, the less oppurtunity there is for true maturity. So we're under the ceiling; all mankind has been under the ceiling. But where are those who will recognize their immaturity, who will recognize that they are actually childish? As I say, we can get big intellectually and big physically but this can act as a facade in relationship to true maturity. The person has this big front but inside he is quite childish. Childishness is usually revealed when a little pressure comes on the person, and then we find out whether there is any maturity or not. A person who is in fact mature will remain himself regardless of the circumstances that present themselves – whether they are good, bad, whatever. Life does not change in the sense of its nature, but the forms which life expresses through are constantly changing. Life is the same today, yesterday and forever, and a person who is identified with life has that experience. His experience is not consequent upon what's going on out in the environment. Those whose identity is still under the ceiling are like a barometer. If they think things are good, they're happy. If they think things are bad, they're sad. All their experience is determined by what's going on in their environment, a sure sign that man is under the ceiling.

To come through that ceiling there must be a recognition of childishness. And you know, we all find ourselves in this boat, probably in varying degrees. However, if human beings are to get on that track again they must recognize they are off the track, quite immature, because to be immature and not recognize it is a fatal state. There's nothing wrong with recognizing immaturity, any more than there is anything wrong with a child being eight years old and having a particular physical form. That's fine. I don't think mother worries about junior growing up when he's eight years old. I have often marveled that a mother is never concerned that her newborn baby will grow up physically. She just takes it for granted. Well, of course!

We can come into this particular state of consciousness where we are truly mature. But, you know, you can't study yourself into this state, you can't wish yourself into this state. The only way you can come into this state is to be identified with the reality which brought up the physical form. How much do you think the average person has matured mentally? Do you think mental maturity comes because you get a lot of knowledge stuffed into your heads? No. You don't take a child and say, 'Now, Junior, we're going to take life away from you, but we're going to send you to school and that will make you grow up physically.' What do you think? It wouldn't work, would it? No. The same reality that allows the physical form to mature allows the mental capacity to develop and allows the emotional capacity to develop. We might say there are various aspects to maturity. There's the physical maturity, and we usually can't interfere with that too much. It proceeds in spite of everything we do. There's a mental maturity, and mental maturity doesn't come because we stuff knowledge in. It comes because of the working of the same reality that allowed the physical form to develop. Maturity does not come by much knowledge. Actually, if we have a mind that has much knowledge and isn't mature we have a very dangerous mind. Even a little knowledge is a dangerous thing when there isn't a mature mind.

And there's another maturity; it's a moral maturity. What's moral maturity? Human beings are always talking about morals. There are those who think they are morally fit. What is a morally fit person? What is morality? Morality is responsibility. A person who is morally mature realizes he or she is responsible for the reality of life to be expressed on earth, taking the attitude 'I am responsible.' And then there's emotional maturity. Emotions really put people on the rocks, don't they? They say, 'Well I can't help what I feel. I can't help getting disturbed. I can't help being depressed. I can't help being upset. I can't help it. I can't help it. I can't help it.' Well it seems sometimes you can't. But the truth is you can, if you understand, if you allow this process to work out.

Finally, we have spiritual maturity. What would spiritual maturity be? Spiritual maturity has something to do with perception, having the ability to perceive spiritually. Spiritual things are spiritually discerned – not physically, not emotionally, but spiritually. A spiritually mature person has allowed the maturing process to come to the point where he or she may discern and perceive from the level which transcends the body with its mind and its emotional realm. Such a person may then be in a position to tap into the source of wisdom, have a sense of the fitness of things, and actually know what he's doing. Now, most people think they know what they're doing. Sometimes a person, having been asked a question, will answer, 'God knows.' That's right, and we may share that knowing, we may share the reality of God's knowing; however, to share that knowing there must be spiritual maturity.

So if we've recognized an immaturity in our own experience the need is to get back on the track. And in order to get back on the track our values need to change. The things that are of true value are not the things of physical form, the things that we can touch. 'Seeing is believing,' we say. No. Value is in the nature of life, and life has a very specific and definite nature. A person who has his values straight is consistently and constantly expressing life's nature. Now most people think that there are circumstances where you can't express life's nature. For instance, there might be circumstances where a particular person said something about you that probably wasn't too nice. Did you ever have anyone do that to you? It wasn't nice, and you're so nice and they talked about you that way! In that particular situation most human beings, all human beings who are under this ceiling, allow what another person says and does to determine what they're going to express. You talk about puppets – Pavlovian dogs! Another person says something about you, and you resent what they say. The bell is rung and you salivate, you resent. A person who has come through the ceiling and realizes that real values are in life's qualities is not going to change his nature or character if someone says something inane but will continue to express the same character and therefore know the experience of life. That person reveals maturity. How wonderful this is, isn't it? Here's something stable. Here's something dependable. Here's something that isn't pushed around by every passing breeze. Here's something that we can depend upon.

I recently read something from the *Boston Herald American*, the January 23 edition, entitled 'Just Laughing Proved a Cure.' Let me read it to you, correlating it with what we're considering:

In the fall of 1964, the highly respected editor of the *Saturday Review*, Norman Cousins, ordered a nurse in a New York hospital instructed in the use of a movie projector so that he could watch old television films of Allen Funt's 'Candid Camera' show every few hours.

Hospitalized with a mysterious joint and connective tissue disease specialists agreed was incurable and would almost certainly permanently cripple him, Cousins did some research of his own and became convinced that positive emotions (joy or glee, for example) and high doses of intravenous Vitamin C were all he needed to become the 'one' in the one in 500 said to recover from his ailment.

He soon took his 'Candid Camera' reruns and his Vitamin C to a hotel room, gave up the aspirin, phenylbutazone, codeine, and sleeping pills prescribed for him at the hospital and, with the help of his physician, set about to heal himself.

Norman Cousins is today free of the collagen disease that had threatened to keep him an invalid, in severe pain, for the rest of his life. He plays Bach fugues, tennis and the typewriter as well as he ever did and in a recent issue of the prestigious *New England Journal of Medicine* writes about laughing his way to health; what he calls the 'chemistry of the will to live.'

Life laughs! What do you think of that? One of the qualities of life is happiness. Life is happy. It has nothing to do with where you are. So many people think they have to be in a particular circumstance in order to be happy. If you have to be in a particular circumstance to be happy you are dying. Life is happy! I used to speak at the prison at Canon City, Colorado, and I remember one day I explained to the prisoners that even a bird would sing in a cage. Of course! The bird in the cage doesn't say, 'Me, sing? I'm all caged up!' He doesn't know any better. He's expressing the qualities of life, and through this little feathered form comes the sound. Life sings!

Isn't it interesting that the moment this man began to even laugh, or express what he called positive emotions – joy and glee – he began to be identified with life. Now this distortion which was presenting itself in his physical form was there because he wasn't allowing his alignment to be with life. Life doesn't give you arthritis. I remember a woman coming under my service at one time who was all crippled up with arthritis and she had a very deep self-pity complex. She said, 'This must be God's will.' I said, 'You can get out of here! Quick! Get out of here!' She said, 'Well . . . well what for?' I said, 'Well if I helped you I would be going against God's will!' God, the author of arthritis? God, the author of cancer? No! Man, the author of arthritis. Man, the author of cancer. Life has a design. When we lose our alignment with life we lose our alignment with life's design. It has a design for this physical body. Take the life out of this body, the design goes. Begin to diminish the expression of life through this form and the distortions in the form begin to show up because the perfect design is contained in life. So here's healing! Human beings want to stay under the ceiling and they want healing for their cancer. They'll spend millions and millions of dollars trying to find a cure for something that of course isn't a problem anyway! There is no such thing as an incurable disease, just incurable human beings! That's what is incurable, not the disease. Do you think this power which took two germs and built a baby couldn't correct any distortion that might be present in the physical form, or in the mental realm, if it were allowed to work unhindered? Human beings want to have their cake and eat it too! They want to stay immature and not have the results of their immaturity. It doesn't work. Let's get on the winning side. Life is a winner. And those who find identity with life begin to have a winning experience.

A cardinal symptom of an immature person is that he is rejecting his present circumstances. He's rejecting them, and his mind is very busy rationalizing why these circumstances are not pleasing to him. He is completely and absolutely deluded! A person who is mature accepts his circumstances; not only does he accept them, he realizes they are the only ones he has. He doesn't have any others! Imagine a pianist who keeps rejecting the piano. He says, 'I'm a pianist, but get that piano out of here.' If a person is going to live he needs circumstances, and these circumstances are our piano. That's what we play the tune of life on. Anyone who is really living, really playing the tune of life, doesn't reject his circumstances. He doesn't say, 'I wish it were different,' or 'Why does this happen to me?' If it is happening to you I would suggest you earned it! How wonderful to forget our circumstances. Who cares about our circumstances? Life is the thing that is important. We have these circumstances so that we might have our values straight and express the qualities of life. And as the qualities of life are expressed and find expression through our outer facilities, particularly our mental and emotional capacities, these capacities continue to develop. They've been thwarted in their development. As life begins to move through the mind consistently it begins to be a brilliant mind. As I've emphasized, a brilliant mind isn't a mind that is stuffed with all kinds of information. If something is brilliant it's lit up. A mind that is lit up is a mind that is expressing life, and one of the qualities of life is light. A person who is expressing life's qualities begins to be enlightened because life is light; life lightens the mind. And the person who is consistent in the expression of life through the emotional capacity – which has been so limited, so restricted – begins to move and expand so that through this emotional capacity the fine nuances and essences of life begin to be sensed, the beautiful reality which stands behind this capacity is sensed. We begin to feel the strength of it, the power of it, the wonder of it, the wisdom of it. Now, can you tell me how anyone could be bored? How anyone could be fed up? How anyone could be depressed?

There are many human beings who are disillusioned. We hear that sometimes. Often in counseling with people they will say, 'Well I'm disillusioned.' I usually say, 'Wonderful! That shows you've had illusions; now you're getting rid of them!' The person had a mental concept of how a certain thing should be and it didn't work out that way. Isn't it wonderful for a person to recognize that he has been disillusioned? That's progress. I would suggest that one of the greatest signs of progress in relationship to the mind is recognizing that what man is trying to do and the way he's doing it on earth is impossible, absolutely impossible. We need those on earth who begin to grow up, not just physically, but grow up in relationship to identity. We need those who come through this fifth door so that identity begins to emerge out of this body, with its mental and emotional capacities, and begins to be centered in the reality which stands behind the physical form. Then there are those who may say in truth, 'I am life. I am come that they might have life more abundantly.' We can say in truth, 'I am life, and I have a body.' Most people say, 'I am a body, and I have life.' No, no. 'I am life, and I have a body'; not 'I am a body, and I have life.' We no longer are separate from life as if it is something we have that we can do what we want with. Life is intelligent, life has a design, and fulfilment on earth may be known only when we allow that design which is inherent in life to come out. To be in line with it, to be aligned with it, we must express its qualities. We must love it; we must love life. I've heard many say, 'Oh I love life,' and yet they go about forfeiting it. If a person loves life he expresses life, and if one is expressing the qualities of life he is revealing maturity on earth.

Let us live. And if we are in fact living, if our cup is running over with life, then we have some life to offer to others. We can't offer life if our cup isn't running over; in such case we're probably running around having others dip a little life into us. We're not here to have others dip life into us. We're here that there might be life and life more abundantly, and in order to offer the reality of life to our brothers and sisters we must have an abundance ourselves. If we are who we are there is always plenty to us; there is lots to go around. If we have that experience we may in fact provide something for others so that they may get on this track again, so that they may mature, so that they may be in expression what they are in reality – LIFE!

A public lecture given in Loveland, Colorado, February 14, 1978.

A FURTHER STEP

The spirit revealed in this book is being recognized as their own by thousands of people throughout the world. It may be that you have sensed this to be true of yourself.

It has proven useful to identify this emerging organism by the name, Society of Emissaries. If you wish to learn more about the approach to living exemplified by this growing body you may do so by writing to:

Society of Emissaries, P.O. Box 238, Loveland, Colorado 80537